PENGUIN METRO READS
CAN'T QUARANTINE OUR LOVE

Sudeep Nagarkar has authored thirteen bestselling novels, including *Few Things Left Unsaid, That's the Way We Met, It Started with a Friend Request, Sorry, You're Not My Type, You're the Password to My Life, You're Trending in My Dreams, She Swiped Right into My Heart, All Rights Reserved For You, Our Story Needs No Filter, She Friend-Zoned My Love, The Secrets We Keep, Stand By Me!* and, his last release, *A Second Chance.*

All his books combined have sold more than a million copies and continue to be on bestseller lists. He has been featured on the *Forbes India* longlist of the most influential celebrities for two consecutive years. He was also awarded the 'Celebrity Author of 2013' title by Amazon. In 2016, he was named the 'Youth Icon of India' by Zee Awards and the 'Best Fiction Novelist of the Year' by WBR Group.

He has given guest lectures at various renowned institutes, including IITs, IIMs and NITs, and has spoken at TEDx.

Connect with Sudeep on social media platforms, where he interacts with more than half a million fans.

Facebook fan page: facebook.com/sudeepnagarkar
Facebook profile: facebook.com/nagarkarsudeep
Twitter handle: @sudeep_nagarkar
Instagram: @SUDEEPNAGARKAR

Can't Quarantine Our Love

Sudeep Nagarkar

Penguin
metro reads

An imprint of Penguin Random House

PENGUIN METRO READS

USA | Canada | UK | Ireland | Australia
New Zealand | India | South Africa | China

Penguin Metro Reads is part of the Penguin Random House group of companies
whose addresses can be found at global.penguinrandomhouse.com

Published by Penguin Random House India Pvt. Ltd
7th Floor, Infinity Tower C, DLF Cyber City,
Gurgaon 122 002, Haryana, India

First published in Penguin Metro Reads by Penguin Random House India 2021

ISBN 9789385990021

Typeset in Adobe Caslon Pro by Manipal Technologies Limited, Manipal
Printed at Thomson Press India Ltd, New Delhi

www.penguin.co.in

Chapter 1

Have you ever taken a flight or a train and immediately plugged in your earphones after boarding? Or have you ever pretended to be sleeping or reading a book just so you can avoid talking to the passenger seated next to you?

Avni has. She would rather write lengthy messages on WhatsApp than pick up the phone and have an actual conversation with someone. She pretends not to see people she knows when she's out in public. I remember her telling me that she once hid in a clothing store inside a mall when she spotted someone she knew. Every quiet girl has a wild side to her, but not Avni. I have always thought of asking her if she ever feels lonely living in her own little bubble, but I know what she'll say—it's better to be on your own than take bullshit from people who

1

merely pretend to care. No one knows her better than me—I've known her since school and she shares all her secrets, big and small, with me. We're best friends and forever companions.

Our friendship goes back years, and by now I know that in spite of her reserved nature, she is beautiful and caring. One of the risks of being quiet is that other people can fill your silence with interpretation. Having faced it often myself, I know when they can't read you, they make up their own story—not always the one we choose or that's true to who we are. But Avni hardly cares, as the four picture frames in our bedroom attest, which define her set rules of life. Her maternal grandmother had left her with a few words of wisdom she swore by. *Never get too attached to someone; always stay focused in life and use your time wisely; beware of your limitations and do only what you're good at; make life better for tomorrow.*

I still remember Avni had come home from school one day and narrated with excitement how the most handsome guy from her school had leaned towards her and confessed that he liked her, to which she hadn't known how to respond. Everyone envied her at the time, but all she wanted to do was run away or vanish into thin air. She found dating books better than dating a boy. You may wonder what kind of an idiot picks books over relationships. But that night, she told me why she did that. Books don't mind if you put them aside for a little bit to focus on yourself. Books don't mind even if you fall asleep on them. And there's no such thing as too many books. You can even read two books or more at the same time, and chances are they will never find out about each other. So why choose a boyfriend over books?

That's Avni for you—her views and opinions in total contrast to her parents' who had a love marriage twenty years ago.

~

It was the wedding anniversary of Avni's parents, and she was busy preparing a big surprise for them. She usually slept in on a Sunday, but today she had woken up early to take printouts of all their photographs together. She was creating a special album for them that would make them relive old memories. She gave the final touch to the album by adding a special note to it.

Dear Mom and Dad,

In spite of the many times you have put me in awkward situations; in spite of being more active on social media than me; and in spite of being naughty in the forties, I love you and I am proud to be your daughter.

Here's wishing you another year of togetherness, and many more to come.

Your little girl forever,
Avni

Just as Avni finished writing the note, she heard loud Punjabi music blasting from the living room and knew that her parents had already started the celebrations. She opened the door of her bedroom to see that they were recording a video blog enthusiastically for their popular YouTube channel 'MC-BC', the acronyms for their names, Mona Chadha and Balwinder Chadha.

Avni's dad said, 'Hi guys, BC and MC are back with a new video. New subscribers, let us start by saying the channel name is not slang. I, Balwinder Chadha, and my wife Mona Chadha, address each other affectionately as MC and BC, and that's how the channel name came to be. Today is a very special day for us because we are celebrating our twentieth anniversary.' He paused and looked at Mona with the same affection he had when they first met, 'Wow, it's been twenty years, is it? Add our dating years and it becomes twenty-five. These years have gone by so quickly, yet we have built so much in this life together. Be it our matrimonial service company Jodi.com, or going on unplanned road trips or playing X-box together, we have lived our moments. Our legacy will be our love for each other, and our daughter, Avni.'

Mona took over. 'Twenty years ago, we became husband and wife. Before that, we were just two kids who were madly in love with each other. We didn't know a lot back then, but we knew one thing for certain, and that was that we belonged together. In the first year of college, when BC proposed to me, I knew he was the one. With him by my side, I can conquer the world. We've been told many times that we can give young couples a run for their money. It's all the love you have for us, dear viewers, that reflects in our relationship.'

Avni was standing near the doorway eavesdropping on them and thinking, *Ya, right. Who knows this better than me?* They were both so engrossed in their video that they didn't realize Avni was already in the living room. The moment they saw her, her dad announced, 'And here's Avni, our lovely daughter . . .'

He turned the camera towards her but before he could add anything and capture her, Avni jumped out of the frame.

'Dad, don't involve me in all this; you know I hate it,' she said irritatedly.

Avni's dad stopped the video recording and walked towards her. Avni was trying to hide the gift-wrapped album behind her but when she saw him approaching, she quickly sat on the sofa and hid the album under her.

Her father sat beside her and said, 'Avni, you should learn to relax now, *bachcha*. You are soon going to go to engineering college. Live it up! Don't be a bore.'

I wouldn't have taken engineering if I had to live it up, would I? thought Avni.

He continued, 'Your mom and I started dating during our first year of college. And now that your college days are beginning, I want you to go out and have all the fun in the world. These years of your life are precious and won't come back. You shouldn't have any regrets later.'

Avni's mom looked at her husband with an expression of annoyance. Not that she didn't want her daughter to go out and live her life, but she wanted her to enjoy her freedom responsibly and with caution.

'Relax, you guys. There's more to life than falling in love,' said Avni.

Avni's father took a deep breath. He knew there was no way he could change Avni's mind. 'You are a replica of your nani.' He turned towards her mother and said in an amused voice, 'MC, look what's happening. We own one of the best matchmaking services in the country, Jodi.com, and our daughter is not interested in finding a match.'

'Can we just end this here,' Avni pleaded. 'It's not about me today. It's your day and I want to make it special for you.'

She stood up and said, 'Happy anniversary to you both. I love you so much.' Saying this, she handed over the gift-wrapped album to them.

'We love you too,' her mother smiled and hugged her.

Her father was about to open the gift but Avni stopped him.

'Not here. I am taking you on a surprise lunch date. You have to open it there. So go get ready!'

~

'Where are we going? You can at least tell us the location, right?' Avni's father asked as he drove his way around the narrow lanes of Mumbai. Being a Sunday, the traffic was comparatively lighter, letting him enjoy the *Aashiqui* film track that transported them back to the 90s.

'What is the big secret?' he asked again after getting no response from Avni.

'I can't tell you where we are going just yet. But post lunch, we are going to meet Nani. She had called some time back,' Avni replied, looking at her phone.

'Okay, Madam. As you say,' he remarked with a sigh, and followed Avni's directions as he drove.

Both Balwinder and Mona were excited about what lay ahead, and occasionally exchanged glances through the rear-view mirror. In the past couple of decades, they had been through so much together. To be honest, 'so much' never does justice to what a couple has actually lived through. Balwinder and Mona had endured the loss of loved ones, had seen each other through the worst of phases, had been through huge financial strains, but the birth of their daughter had overpowered everything else. They were reminiscing about the old days while Avni was shifting uncomfortably in her seat, nervous about how her parents would react to her surprise.

They were in south Bombay by now, and as they reached closer to the destination, both Balwinder and Mona began guessing possible locations. Soon they found themselves opposite the Metro theatre.

'Here we are. I hope you remember this place?' Avni announced, and gestured to her father to park the car.

As they got out of the car, they found themselves standing outside Kyati & Co, the café where Balwinder had proposed to Mona twenty-five years ago. They hadn't visited the place in years. Soon after Avni was born, they had shifted to the suburbs. But now, standing outside the iconic café, they realized nothing really had changed about the place.

'Wow, it still looks the same to me,' Balwinder said, gazing at the building.

'Indeed. Gosh, it all seems like such a long time ago,' Mona added with a big smile on her face.

They hugged Avni and thanked her for the surprise as they entered the café. The architecture, the walls, the tables looked the same. Nothing much had changed.

'That's our table,' Balwinder said in delight, pointing towards the table at the extreme end.

Avni could see her mom blushing and started to tease her.

Since the table was already occupied, the manager showed them to another vacant table nearby, but they would have none of it.

'That's the table where I had proposed to my wife so you will understand why, on our twenty-fifth wedding anniversary, we can't sit on any other table except that one. We will wait, thank you,' he said, taking Mona's hand in his. She responded by kissing his hand, much to the delight of the waiters around them.

'Mom . . . Dad . . . please, you're embarrassing me! Stop acting like two love-struck teenagers. You're forgetting you're both well over forty.'

'What does age have to do with love? You should feel embarrassed when I'm hugging some other woman instead of your mother,' he said with a cheeky expression.

'Very funny,' Avni said.

After a few minutes of waiting, they were finally directed to *their* table. The manager even brought a complimentary pastry for them.

'A little token of love from our side, for being such loyal patrons of our café.'

They thanked the manager for the sweet gesture and once he left, Avni handed over the gift to her parents. Balwinder and Mona were amazed at the efforts their daughter had put behind it. It's the little memories that last a lifetime, and she had gifted a collection of all the memories they had made together. They were overwhelmed by it all. Mona had tears in her eyes as she scrolled through each photograph. After reading the special note, she held Avni's hand and said, 'We are really blessed to have a daughter like you. May God give you all the happiness in life.'

'I love you, Mom and Dad,' Avni replied, enveloping them in a hug.

Avni's world revolved around her family. They meant everything to her and she could do anything to see them smile. As her dad looked through the photographs, something struck him. He picked up the pastry on the table and looked straight into Mona's eyes. Then he stood up and went down on his knees, holding out his hand with the pastry offering before her. He was recreating the day he had proposed to her.

'Time and time again I have tried to put into words how I feel for you. But as we enter our twentieth year together as husband and wife, all I can say is that I love you, my darling MC.'

Mona took a small bite of the pastry. She was speechless and didn't know how to react. But the blush on her face and the sparkle in her eyes gave her emotions away. Suddenly the room echoed with the sound of loud clapping. Their fellow diners had risen from their seats and were hooting and cheering them on. Avni was a little embarrassed by it. She absolutely detested their public display of affection. She wondered how, in spite of having parents who loved each other so much, she was so averse to even the idea of love. She wondered if she could ever love someone as much as they loved each other. After much contemplation, she came to the same conclusion she always did—that love wasn't her cup of tea.

~

On Sundays, Mumbaikars feel at peace while driving on the roads, but for someone who's coming from outside Mumbai, it's still a pain to drive because of the numerous road blocks at regular intervals. Sidharth's family found itself in a similar situation. They were shifting from Surat to the suburbs of Mumbai, and were on their way to their new home in the cab while a truck of Movers & Packers with all their belongings trailed them. Sidharth had secured admission in a college in Mumbai. He wanted to pursue engineering through AIEEE and thus, despite loving Surat, Sidharth's mother,

Anandiben Shah, had to shift with him along with Sidharth's maternal grandfather, Mansukbhai. Ever since his parents' divorce, Sidharth had become the biggest priority for his mother.

'How much more time will it take to reach?' she asked the cab driver.

'Google Maps says half an hour tops,' he replied.

'My Surat is way better than Mumbai; look at the condition of the roads here! There are so many potholes that I feel like I am on a roller coaster. Sidharth, why did you have to choose to do your engineering in Mumbai? Couldn't you have picked another city?'

Sidharth was gazing outside the window, lost in his thoughts. His grandfather was sitting next to him, his complete attention on an intimate scene being played out on a new *Game of Thrones* episode he was watching on his phone.

'Wow,' he exclaimed suddenly.

'What wow?' Sidharth's mother turned around. 'Papa, are you watching your idiotic movies again?'

Sidharth's grandfather panicked and immediately locked his screen, 'No . . . not at all. I was saying this city is just wow. You are cribbing unnecessarily. Now that we are here at last, give the city a chance. I've heard that people in Mumbai are progressive, much like the United States. They call it the New York of India.'

As he spoke to his daughter, all Nana really wanted to do was go back to watching the movie. She would have been dismayed to know that. She knew that every night after she went to sleep, he would put on American films and enjoy a drink while watching them. A retired jailor, he had moved in with his daughter to help her after she separated from Sidharth's father. His jovial nature really helped uplift the mood in the house. Every time Anandiben would feel low, he would encourage her to start her life afresh. He was very close to his grandson—he was more of a friend than a grandfather to Sidharth. They kept no secrets from each other, and Sidharth kept him up-to-date on the latest movies.

As the cab neared their destination, Sidharth wondered how his college life would turn out to be. He always imagined college to be straight out of a Bollywood movie— cute girls lining the hallways and boys vrooming in on their bikes.

Coincidentally, their car was passing by a college, and his mother was aghast to see rowdy teenagers milling about outside the gates, with little decorum being displayed in their behaviour with one another.

'You were right, Papa. This generation is way too advanced,' she said, her remark intended for Sidharth. When she got no response from him, she turned to see him lost in thought. 'Sidharth, are you listening to me?'

'Ya . . . ya . . . I am listening. Continue with your lecture, ' he said with irritation.

That irked his mother even further, 'Lecture? You think all this is cool?'

'When did I say that, Mom?'

Parents are sometimes no less than TV journalists. They just put words in your mouth and then keep debating as if the nation wants to know who's right. The nation doesn't give a fuck.

'Sidharth, these kids are just wasting their time and their parents' money. I don't want you to turn into one of them. I hope you won't get too spoilt here in Mumbai.'

'Don't worry, Mom. I'm not going to turn into one of them. And anyway, I'm not into girls.'

'What do you mean by that?' Nana asked.

'I mean not for now at least. I need to concentrate on my studies.'

'You almost gave me a heart attack by saying you don't like girls,' he chided Sidharth. 'Don't worry Anandi beta, he knows his responsibilities. He is now an adult and can differentiate between right and wrong. And he has always been a rank holder.'

'I know. I just fear for him so much. We have done everything possible to give him the best life we could,' Sidharth's mother said. 'We have been living only on my fixed deposits and your pension. If your friend hadn't given his vacant house in Mumbai to us on rent, it would have been really tough for us. I have gone through so much already, and I cannot let anything come in Sidharth's way. I just want him to be well settled and live a happy life.'

'Mom, stop worrying so much. Everything will fall into place. And instead of telling Nana to stop watching the films he likes, you should perhaps stop watching the crime shows that fill your head with negative thoughts,' Sidharth concluded.

Sidharth was reckless and carefree by nature, but he didn't ever let that come in the way of his studies. He was a brilliant student, and like any other kid his age, he loved to go out with his friends. By now he was used to his mother's constant worrying, and took it lightly because he knew she had his best interests at heart. Sidharth took a deep breath and got ready to welcome his new life in Mumbai.

~

After having lunch in the café, Avni and her parents had come to meet Nani, who stayed a couple of blocks away from their house. There was not a day when Avni didn't come to meet her. Her mother would always say that Nani was happiest when Avni was around. Avni too shared a strong emotional bond with her grandmother, and always sought her guidance in matters close to her heart.

'So what gift do you want on your anniversary?' Nani asked Balwinder after he took her blessings.

'Will you really give us what I ask?' Balwinder asked cheekily.

Nani had a fairly good idea about what he would say. It was always the same thing. He asked, 'Will you move in with us? We've been asking you for a really long time! If you say yes, that would be the best gift for us today.'

Avni instantly jumped at the suggestion and remarked excitedly, 'That's the best gift indeed. Nani, what's the point in us staying so close to each other and still not be together?'

Nani smiled and said, 'You are there for me and that's all that matters. You see, it's not so easy for me to give up this house—every corner has Nana's memories attached to it. And how can I stay at my son-in-law's house? That is not okay in our family. What will people think?'

Who cares what people think? That's the reason I hate this concept of marriage and moving into another household. How can one separate a daughter from her parents?

'To hell with such traditions, Nani. Who believes in such things in today's times?' Avni said in frustration. It wasn't going to be easy to convince her grandmother.

Balwinder and Mona stood there silently. They knew she wouldn't change her mind. It had been years since they had been pleading with her, but she always gave the same reply.

'You are just one call away. I can call you if I need anything.' Eventually, even Avni gave up. They spent some time together and then left.

As they entered their lane, they saw a truck parked right next to their house.

'It seems like the new tenants have moved in,' Balwinder remarked.

When they reached their gate, they saw a lady arguing with a cab driver.

'Why should I leave the thirty rupees? You should be carrying spare change with you. We have already paid you extra for the luggage and now this trickery.'

'Madam, I don't have change. You give me twenty rupees and I'll give you fifty back. You can check my wallet if you don't believe me,' the cab driver said.

It was Sidharth's mother. Sidharth and Nana were busy helping the delivery boys unload the boxes, but when he heard the driver and his mother arguing, Sidharth stepped in and asked his mother to let the matter be. But she was adamant and not ready to back off. Balwinder had overheard her conversation with the cab driver, and decided to help out.

'Hi, I'm Balwinder. We stay in the house next door. Can I help you in any way?'

Sidharth's mother looked at him suspiciously. Then she simply nodded and looked away. Nana walked up to Balwinder and extended his hand to greet him warmly.

'Hello, it's nice to meet you. We just shifted here from Surat. That's my daughter. And you know how women are—they can initiate arguments at the drop of a hat!'

'I live with two ladies in the house, so I can totally understand. There they are, seated in the car,' Balwinder said, pointing towards his car. Mona waved from inside. Balwinder said, 'So you're from Gujarat? Gujjus are known to be penny pinchers, no? I have heard stories of how Gujjus don't compromise on even a single rupee.'

Sidharth's mother shot him a look of annoyance, but Nana laughed.

'Yeah, we're the opposite of Punjabis. You guys should take tips from us on how to save for a rainy day,' said Nana.

He then introduced himself. 'I am Mansukbhai, a retired jailor.'

Balwinder shook hands with him and said, 'It's great meeting you, Jailor Sahib.'

Anandiben, who was hearing their conversation, now spoke up. 'Can we resolve the cab issue first?'

Meanwhile, Sidharth, who had seen Avni sitting in the car, could not take his eyes off her, and was not listening to the conversation. He had never seen anyone so beautiful! Avni was busy on her phone and paid him no attention. And when she did look up in his direction fleetingly, his heart skipped a beat. Embarrassed to have been caught staring, he quickly averted his gaze and pretended to lift one of their many boxes. But as soon as Avni looked away, he couldn't help but stare at her again.

He was smitten! He didn't even realize when Avni's dad handed over the change to the cab driver and put an end to the matter. It was only when his mother asked him to help her take the luggage inside that he reluctantly looked at her. The house help, who was waiting for them, helped bring the other boxes inside. Once everything was in the house, Sidharth hurried out to see if Avni was still around, but she had gone.

He was waiting by the door with a dejected look on his face when his grandfather tapped him on the shoulder.

'What happened, boy? What are you waiting here for?'

'No, nothing. I just wanted to thank our new neighbours for all their help,' Sidharth replied sheepishly.

Sidharth's mom remarked, 'Stop making a big deal about it. The help wasn't needed. And why are we trusting complete strangers? We know nothing about them. They could be murderers for all we know.'

Murderers? What is mom even saying? I think I need to cancel her Netflix subscription.

After a couple of hours, when the unpacking had been done, Sidharth went to check out his room's balcony. As he stood marvelling the Mumbai skyline from his apartment, he realized his balcony faced Avni's window. He could see her sitting there. Looking at her made his heart race. How could he feel such a magnetic pull towards a person so soon? She hadn't even spoken a word to him.

Avni, lost in her thoughts, suddenly saw Sidharth through her bedroom window.

Isn't he the boy from downstairs? Why the hell is he staring at me like a maniac?

Sidharth mustered some courage and tried nodding at her casually, but his face broke into a sudden smile. To his surprise, she smiled back at him. He couldn't believe his eyes. He wanted to run to her but all he could do was stand there and stare. Finally, somewhat irritated by his gaze, Avni drew the curtains briskly.

Fuck, what have I done? I've made such a bad first impression. What would she be thinking about me? Did she really smile or was I hallucinating? I'm such a fool. I have to do better tomorrow. Can't wait to see what Mumbai has in store for me!

And with those thoughts his head, Sidharth crashed on the bed after what had been a long, adventurous day indeed.

Chapter 2

Why I am finding it hard to stop thinking about her? Why are my thoughts headed in only her direction? I hardly know her; I've barely seen her; so where are these feelings coming from? What is happening to me?

Sidharth's head was swarming with a million unanswered questions as he made his way towards the grocery store, which was located a couple of lanes away from his house. In his hand was the list of grocery items his mother had asked him to buy. Once he reached the store, he took out the list and handed it over to the shopkeeper, who was chatting with another customer. The shopkeeper went through the list and looked up at Sidharth.

'So you've just moved into this neighbourhood, right?'

'Yes, a short while ago,' Sidharth replied adjusting the sleeves of his shirt.

'We've also started home delivery, in case you prefer that,' the shopkeeper replied as he instructed one of the boys in his shop to get the things on the list.

'Sure, I'll let you know,' Sidharth replied as he casually glanced around.

'Where are you from? You don't look like you're from here,' asked the other customer.

'We've moved here from Surat, Gujarat, since I've recently secured admission in a college in Mumbai.'

'Isn't Chadha's daughter too entering her first year of graduation?' he asked the shopkeeper as he packed away the list of items in a bag.

'Yes, her father had even distributed sweets on her admission. I wish she had fed me with her own hands though. God, she's turned into a real beauty, hasn't she?'

The other customer stopped him short and said, 'Don't talk nonsense about her. She's your bhabhi.'

'Yeah, right. As if she has no other work except to wait at home for your proposal.'

Sidharth was disgusted with their exchange. Two middle-aged men saying such rubbish about a girl before another customer! Had they no shame?

'Oh did you happen to see Chadha's daughter this morning? They live in the house exactly opposite yours,' the shopkeeper asked.

Sidharth had to put an end to their rude conversation. 'What is wrong with you two? How can you talk like this about a girl half your age? Don't you have wives and sisters at home? If her father finds out about the stuff you guys have been saying about his daughter behind his back, he will skin you both alive.'

And with that, he stormed out of the store.

As he reached outside his gate, he looked up at his neighbour's house, expecting Avni to be standing by her window, but there was no one.

He entered his house, handed over the grocery bag to his mom dejectedly and went to the washroom. He had barely locked the door when he heard his mother calling out to him. *Can't a boy even pee in peace now?* He hurried out and went straight to the kitchen where his mother was standing with a stern look on his face.

'Didn't I clearly write in the list that you had to bring Amul full-cream milk? And what have you got?' she asked accusatorily handing him another brand's tetra pack. 'Also, where's the curd I had asked you to get? I don't see it anywhere. And why are you so lost today?'

Those rascals at the shop. They've completely messed this up! I knew they weren't to be trusted with the list. And what do I tell Mom now? That I was too busy fighting with them over a girl I haven't even met to check the list properly?

Sidharth had no choice but to lie.

'That brand wasn't available so I got the best substitute I could find. I can go back and return it if you want.'

His reply pacified her a little. 'No, it's fine. I am going to a temple nearby. I'll see what can be done when I'm back.'

'Temple? Wouldn't it be closed during the afternoons? And why are you going out in this sweltering heat?' asked Nana as he entered the kitchen.

'It's Sunday. Most temples are open all day on Sundays,' she replied. 'And I have to seek God's blessings before we embark on our new journey. Plus Sidharth's college starts tomorrow.'

'Mom, I think you should rest for now. It's been a long and tiring journey, and I think God will understand if you visit him a day or two later.'

'Sidharth, let her go. You can't change anyone's beliefs. If she finds solace in God, then let her go and get his blessings. You can't fight everything with logic,' explained Nana.

Sidharth looked incredulous. *How had Nana turned religious all of a sudden?*

Once his mother had left for the temple, Sidharth opened the YouTube app on his phone to watch a few videos on engineering to keep his mind occupied and away from any lingering thoughts of Avni. But the top search results only threw up results like

'Life of an unemployed engineer' and 'Why engineers are a frustrated bunch', which irritated him. Eventually, he clicked on a video whose title made him feel better: 'The amazing life of a mechanical engineer.' He played the video and the voice-over began:

Before we start the video, let me tell you that I am an accidental mechanical engineer. Yes, you heard me right. And till today, I have been searching for those people who had once told me, 'Engineering has a lot of scope.' Let me tell you guys, during your mechanical engineering college years, you learn everything apart from your core course studies. You learn that interacting with girls is a rare phenomenon since the mechanical branch barely has any girls. And this is how porn becomes your best friend. When you're not watching porn, you spend your time on movies and equip yourself with useless knowledge that will not secure you any job post your graduation.

Sidharth took the video seriously, not realizing that the YouTuber was only trying to be sarcastic. Bummed at the uncertainty of his future, he shut down his laptop and walked towards the window. As he glanced at the road below, he saw a courier boy standing outside Chadha's house with a bouquet of flowers. Sidharth hoped and prayed they weren't for her.

Maybe he is at the wrong address? Or maybe those are for her mother?

As Sidharth came up with multiple theories about the flowers, he saw Avni opening the door. She exchanged a few words with the delivery guy, who handed the bouquet over to her and left.

Are the flowers from her boyfriend? Of course, why can't she have one? She is beautiful and young. But why would her boyfriend send the flowers to her house instead of giving them to her. No, I am just overthinking. She is obviously single.

Sidharth felt a tap on his shoulder. It was Nana.

'I've been calling you from the living room for the last five minutes.'

'Sorry, I was thinking about something,' Sidharth replied sheepishly. 'Do you need something?'

His grandfather had a mischievous glint in his eyes, 'Since you're asking, I'd like an Old Monk quarter. Please buy me one before your Mom comes home. Now that we have settled into our new place, I want to just relax tonight with a peg of rum and a nice movie.'

'Ah, no wonder you wanted Mom to visit the temple.'

'You know your nana,' he winked.

'No Nana, I am not going to bring you one. You're going to get me into so much trouble one day! If you want it, then go get it yourself.'

'Please beta.'

'No "please". I have never gone to a wine shop before. I'm still underage and I doubt they will even let me buy one. It's not Surat, you know.'

Since alcohol is banned in Gujarat, back home in Surat, Sidharth would procure alcohol for him on the sly from Nana's jailor friends. After much coaxing, Sidharth finally relented. He put on a clean tee, took money from his grandfather, and shoved it into his wallet. He then took his backpack to carry the liquor bottle.

He turned the keys in the ignition of his bike only to realize the bike wouldn't start. He pulled the choke and tried again but nothing happened. He got off the bike to check the wiring, but everything seemed okay. He looked in the direction of Avni's window, hoping to spot her, but there was no one.

It's just not my day. Now even my bike refuses to go to a daru shop.

As he tried once again to rev up his bike, he heard the loud honking of a car behind him. He turned around to see Avni's parents in the car and got a shock.

Fuck, did they see me stalking their daughter? Can this day get any worse? He was still cursing when he saw Avni's dad pulling down the car window. He was signalling to him but Sidharth couldn't figure out what he meant. Balwinder spoke up,

'Any problem, beta?'

'No . . . nothing . . . I was just . . .' Sidharth stammered. He didn't know what to say. Balwinder asked him the same question again and somehow this time, he gathered courage to speak.

'My bike . . . it just won't start.'

'Do you want us to drop you somewhere?' Balwinder asked.

Sidharth saw the quizzical look on Avni's mother's face and sensed she wasn't really comfortable with the idea. So he politely declined the offer but Balwinder kept insisting.

'Come in, we will drop you midway to your destination at least. It's absolutely no problem.'

Sidharth realized Balwinder wasn't going to back off so he finally relented and got inside the car. He felt nervous and tried to deflect attention from them by pretending to be on his phone. Balwinder looked at him through the rear-view mirror.

'So where are you headed exactly?'

The question caught him completely off guard. He pretended to be on a call to buy himself a little more time before he answered.

Shit! What do I tell him? I can't say I am headed towards a liquor shop to buy booze for my nana. Their daughter already thinks I am an asshole, and now them. Nanaji, what position have you put me into?! Oh wait, I got it.

'Actually . . . I was looking for a pharmacy. I needed to buy some medicines for my nana. If you can . . .'

Phew, another hurdle crossed. What a roller-coaster of a morning it's been, I feel like I am in the middle of a solo vs squad game in PUBG, barely surviving every damn zone.

'Sure, there's a medical shop nearby. I'll drop you there.'

Sidharth thanked him and went back to his phone to avoid any further conversation. No one spoke for the next few minutes. Eventually, Avni's mother broke the awkward silence.

'So, what about your father? He didn't shift here with you? I didn't spot him in the morning.'

Sidharth replied in a heavy voice. 'My parents are separated. He doesn't stay with us any more.'

Avni's mother felt bad for having asked such a personal question and apologized for the intrusion. 'Oh, I am so sorry. I shouldn't have asked . . .'

'No, I am fine.'

Avni's dad was about to say something when his phone buzzed. It was a friend who had called to wish him happy anniversary.

'Thank you, Saxena. Thanks a lot, dost. *Abhi to ham jawan hain*,' he replied with a hearty laugh.

Sidharth was trying to listen to the person on the other end of the line, but he was not clearly audible in the din of the traffic.

Avni's dad rolled up the windows and continued. 'Can't today. My daughter has planned a party for us tonight and she has asked us not to make any plans. She has been out all day with her friend to prepare for the evening. But I promise, we will make a plan for this week sometime. I'll throw a grand party for our anniversary. That's my promise.'

Sidharth breathed a sigh of relief.

Oh so those flowers were an anniversary present! And not from her boyfriend.

Avni's dad stopped the car outside a pharmacy. 'Here's the medical shop.'

Sidharth wanted to wish them a happy anniversary but hesitated. He didn't know them too well so it might have seemed a bit weird. He got out of the car and politely thanked them for the ride.

Avni's dad bid him goodbye and continued his conversation on the mobile. Sidharth walked towards the medical shop hoping they would drive away so he could change his route. But they had parked outside the pharmacy. Clearly they would not drive away till the phone call was done. Sidharth was in a fix. He had no option but to enter the pharmacy. There were barely any people inside. Sidharth pretended to look for something in the cosmetics section as he peered outside through the glass door, waiting for them to leave. One of the staff members saw Sidharth looking for something. He approached him.

'Are you looking for something in particular, Sir?'

'No, nothing. I was just . . .' Sidharth paused. 'I am good, don't worry.'

The staff member continued to ask him, making Sidharth feel uncomfortable. 'Oh, okay. I got it. Let me help you,' said the assistant.

'Sorry, what do you mean?' Sidharth asked.

'Guys your age come to a medical shop looking for only one thing.'

Sidharth hadn't a clue about what he meant. The man went towards the other side of the counter and reached into a shelf. He placed a few packets of condoms on the counter and winked at Sidharth.

'Which flavour do you prefer?'

'Um, excuse me? I don't need it.' Sidharth turned around to see Balwinder's car had left. It was his cue to exit the pharmacy.

'But Sir, at your age you should be using protection,' the staff member protested as Sidharth made a dash for the exit.

He stepped out and was about to turn left when he saw Avni's parents' car approaching him again.

Now what? Am I after their daughter or are they after me?

The car stopped in front of him and Balwinder got out of the car. As he walked towards him, his heart started beating faster.

'You forgot your phone in our car,' Balwinder said, handing over the phone to him. *Oh shit! I must have dropped it when I exited the car.*

'Thanks a lot, Uncle. I completely forgot about it,' Sidharth said inspecting his phone.

'Hope you got the medicines you were looking for?' he asked.

'Yes, I did,' Sidharth lied, hoping Balwinder wouldn't ask him to show the medicines now.

'Okay then, take care.'

They were about to drive away when Sidharth called out, 'By the way, a very happy marriage anniversary.'

That put a smile on their faces. They thanked him and drove away.

How many boys can claim to not only fall in love but also take a ride with the girl's parents on the same day? he thought, and smiled to himself. It had been a most unusual day indeed.

~

'Sonal, where are you? I've been waiting for you for ages. You better have a good excuse for being late this time,' said Avni.

In spite of their different personalities, Sonal and Avni had been the best of friends since their school days. Between them, they had only one thing in common— both were brilliant in studies. But while Sonal was a quick learner, Avni had to study for hours to get good grades. Avni had called up Sonal since they were supposed to go to the market to pick up stuff for the party later in the evening. But Sonal was late as usual.

'I am almost there. And it's hardly been twenty minutes. I'll tell you the whole story when I come.'

'Stop lying, Sonal. I know you very well. Even if you are in bed in your night clothes, you'll say you are almost there. You and your stories,' Avni sighed. 'I want you here asap, yaar. There's so much to be done.'

By the time Sonal reached the shop, Avni had already driven there on her scooty and bought everything needed for the party.

'Okay, first hear me out before you start blasting me. I broke up with that dumbass last night. And he's been irritating me with calls and messages since the morning. He told me he didn't wish to commit to me. And when I said "okay, fine, let's go our separate ways", he went all crazy. I mean, what does he want exactly?'

'Don't you get tired chasing after guys? I have forgotten the number of times you've broken up by now. It's time you stop and get a life,' Avni said with a straight face.

'You've never been in a relationship, so how would you know what it feels like?' Sonal said defending her actions.

'I know what it feels like by seeing you. You're either crying over fights or showing your annoyance over the same fights. I look at you and feel happy over my single status.'

'Forget it. There's no point in telling you . . . Anyway, are you done buying all the things needed for tonight?'

Avni nodded. 'Then let's have some pani puri at our favourite haunt? Leave your scooty here.'

Fight or no fight, Avni couldn't resist the temptation of pani puri. They began walking towards the pani puri stall, talking about college starting the next day. As they neared the stall, Avni saw Sidharth exiting the liquor shop located exactly behind the stall.

'Oh God, what is he doing here?' she exclaimed and turned around quickly to avoid being spotted.

Sonal had a confused look on her face.

'Do you know this guy?'

'Ya, he is our new neighbour. Come, let's hide behind this car.'

'But why? He is so handsome! Why are you avoiding him? You should go ahead and meet him, silly,' Sonal replied, her eyes still locked on Sidharth.

'Handsome? Not at all. And what is he doing buying liquor this early in the morning? Is he even allowed to, at his age?'

'You are so lame. Let me talk to him.' Sonal started walking towards Sidharth, who still hadn't seen the girls.

Before Avni could pull Sonal back, she called him out, 'Hey . . .'

Sidharth, who thought that he had escaped the worst after the ride with Avni's parents, felt a tsunami crashing on to him upon seeing Avni.

Fuck, this can't be real. Am I hallucinating again?

Seeing Sidharth's dazed expression, Sonal snapped her fingers at him, 'Oh hello, I am talking to you.'

The shit is real. I wish I had refused Nana, and never left the safety of my house.

'Hi,' he responded with visible unease.

'So you're her new neighbour then, aren't you?'

'Yes,' Sidharth replied and glanced at Avni, who didn't look too pleased to see him.

'Great to meet you. And I hope to see you around more often,' Sonal replied.

Sidharth wondered if Avni had seem him exiting a liquor shop. *Will she think I'm an alcoholic before I've even got a chance to speak with her? Should I tell her that I was buying liquor for Nana and not for myself. No, she won't believe me. And it will make me seem too desperate to prove that I don't drink.*

He decided to stay quiet and saw Avni pulling Sonal away. They were about to leave when Sidharth called out.

'Have fun at your party tonight.'

Avni simply walked off, desperate to get away from him. She thought he was a complete psycho. And how did he know that there was a party at her home?

When Sidharth reached home, he handed over the Old Monk bottle to his grandfather, much to his delight. But his mind was on his encounter with Avni. More often than not, the first impression is the last impression. And Sidharth had failed miserably in creating one. So what did the future have in store for them?

Chapter 3

It was Avni's first day at engineering college, and she was a bundle of nerves. She had worked hard to secure admission in that college, and making it there was like a dream come true for her. She was so excited that she had gotten up way before time to get dressed for her first day.

'I hope you are all geared up?' her mother asked as she served her an aloo paratha laced with butter at the breakfast table.

'Totally, Mom,' Avni replied. She took a bite of her paratha and texted Sonal to find out what time she was coming to pick her up.

Avni didn't want to be late on the very first day of college. Like any other newcomer, she was both nervous and excited. She had planned to reach college at 10 a.m., and knowing Sonal's utter lack of preparedness and time management, she had texted her to meet a few minutes earlier. Avni was happy for two reasons. One, she had got admission in her dream college, and second, her bestie was going to be with her for the next four years. In a new world full of strangers, it was comforting to know that she had at least one person on her team. Most engineering students are coaxed into it by their parents, but Avni's case was different. Her father wanted her to enter the Arts field so that she could take over Jodi.com in the future, but Avni always dreamt of becoming an engineer.

'Avni, I wish you all the success and I am really happy that you chose your dream stream though you know I wasn't totally in favour of it,' said Balwinder. 'But just don't become a bank manager, writer or anything not related to engineering, like most engineers do.' He laughed.

'Dad, that's not funny. There are good job opportunities if you have the desired skillset. And maybe those people didn't want to become engineers in the first place.'

'You may be right. But according to a recent study, by the year 2050, India will have more engineers than any other country in the world.'

'I can't tell if you're boosting my morale or deflating it?'

'I am just stating facts.'

'Trust me, engineering isn't so easy that just anyone can obtain a degree in it.'

'Ya, for engineering students, every course except engineering is a cake walk.'

The debate wouldn't have ended had Avni's mother not intervened, 'Are you both on a primetime news channel right now? You need to save this debate for later or Avni will get late for college.' She gave her daughter a peck on the cheek and wished her good luck. 'You go, rock star.'

'Of course, she'll rock. She's my daughter, after all,' her dad beamed with pride and gave her a high-five.

After breakfast, she bid goodbye to her parents and left for her grandmother's house, where she had asked Sonal to meet her. She wanted to see Nani before heading to college. There was no way she was starting this new chapter in her life without Nani's blessings. At Nani's, she met Sonal, and they headed to college. On the way, Sonal asked, 'I am a little worried. What if we get ragged on the first day itself? How do we save ourselves from the seniors?'

'Just find some good-looking seniors and make friends with them like you always do,' Avni teased.

'I am serious, Avni. I have heard such horror stories about ragging in engineering colleges. They are the absolute worst.'

'Then haven't you also heard stories that there are anti-ragging cells in college where you can complain about such hooligans?'

'Oh c'mon, who complains on the first day? Anyway, I am just keeping my fingers crossed that we don't get picked on,' Sonal said.

The college wasn't too far from Avni's house and they reached on time. She parked her scooty in the two-wheeler parking space and they entered the premises, where a huge standee was placed. It said 'DC College of Engineering welcomes all first-year students!'

All freshers were asked to gather at the quadrangle, where the timetables and class allotment lists were displayed. The mechanical branch was allotted S3. It had only one section, so Avni and Sonal didn't have to feel worried about getting separate sections, like computers and electronics had to. Sonal was going through the subject list.

'These are too complicated. Why can't they keep it simple? And who the fuck teaches the outdated C and C++ languages? If they have to teach computers to a mechanical student, why can't they include Java or android development skills?'

'Are you done? Now can we go to our classes?'

'I detest the Indian education system. The syllabus is obsolete—it will still rule us for years to come, perhaps for more years than the British monarchy.'

'Have you not evolved after even a dozen break-ups?' said Avni.

Sonal rolled her eyes at Avni. 'Now what do my relationships have to do with my education? You are crazy.'

They went to their classroom, which was on the second floor. Both Avni and Sonal kept teasing and insulting each other. They knew it was all in jest.

~

Today marks a new chapter in my life. A new beginning in a new place, with new friends and a new focus. Wish me luck!

Sidharth uploaded the status on his Facebook profile, and rushed to college on his now repaired Karizma sports bike after his mother had given him a long list of instructions. He was already late and had to navigate using Google maps since he was new to the city. The potholes, the crazy traffic—he was oblivious to it all in the excitement of going to college. A college straight out of a Karan Johar movie.

But the moment he reached the campus, all his expectations collapsed like a pack of cards. The campus was dull-looking, with nerdy students engrossed in their notes or simply doing nothing. No one took any notice of him.

Now I know why they never make movies on actual engineering colleges. Because there is nothing fun here.

Sidharth walked towards the quadrangle to check where the classes were being held. He had a look at the noticeboard and it read 'S3'. He asked a few students where S3 was, and was guided to the second floor. It was already 10:40 a.m. by the time he reached. The lecture was about to end but he managed to sneak into the class from the back door and take a seat on the last bench. The professor was giving an orientation lecture and, while he talked, Sidharth surveyed the room for girls. Sadly, there were very few and he could count them on his fingertips.

What the fuck. The YouTuber was right! Whoever thinks India's sex ratio is a problem has never seen the classroom of a mechanical engineering course.

He looked at the guy sitting beside him, who was making notes of the orientation lecture.

Like seriously? Who does that?

Just then he caught a glimpse of a girl sitting a few rows ahead of him. He knew that face all too well. It was Avni. He couldn't believe his luck! The college that he found gloomy had suddenly turned interesting. He didn't care about the sex ratio any more. He didn't care if there weren't any other girls in the entire college, let alone his class. Avni was here!

Sonal was sitting next to Avni and talking animatedly with her. She said something that made Avni smile. Seeing her, Sidharth started smiling too. He must have looked like a complete idiot staring at her like that, but he didn't care.

It feels like rain in summertime. Should I talk to you after the lecture? Heck, I don't even know your name yet! So how could I be falling for you this bad?

'Sidharth Shah . . . Sidharth . . . is he present?' the professor's voice jolted Sidharth back to reality. He had not heard a word of the lecture so far.

When he realized the professor was taking attendance, he stood up instinctively. He wanted Avni to notice him. He wanted her to turn back and realize how destiny was bringing them together time and again. But she sat unmoved, reading something from the book in front of her. To catch her attention, Sidharth said loudly, 'Yes, Sir.'

But Avni didn't bother to turn around.

'Why are you yelling? This is not a military school. This is an engineering college.'

'Sorry, Sir,' Sidharth replied and sat down. He waited for her to respond to her name-call so he could find out her name. He desperately wanted to know it and couldn't wait any longer. Finally, it came.

'Avni Chadha.'

'Present, Sir,' she replied.

Avni. Avni and Sidharth! That had a nice ring to it.

The lecture got over but before the students could take a breather, the maths professor entered the class. He introduced himself and started discussing his subject. Just then, a girl entered from the back door and sat beside

Sidharth. All the seats in the classroom were taken by then and that was the only vacant place left.

'Hi, I'm Bani,' she introduced herself with confidence.

'I'm Sidharth.'

'I missed my first lecture. Did the guy discuss anything important?'

'You think? Lectures are just for the sake of attendance!'

'I agree,' she laughed.

They started chatting like old friends. As he was talking to her, he thought about how it had never been a problem for him to talk to girls. So why did the thought of talking to Avni make him speechless? As they continued to take full advantage of the last bench, Sidharth noticed Bani's attire. She was wearing a striped shirt with tattered black jeans and boots. Her hair was in a messy bun, and besides kajal, she wore no other make-up. He could tell she didn't bother too much about her looks, and was like one of the boys.

After completing his orientation, the professor announced, 'So, students, I am calling out the three toppers of this class. I have your details, including your HSC (Higher Secondary Board) and entrance marks. According to that, the top three students have to come forward and solve a simple mathematical equation that you have already studied during your entrance test. It's just to evaluate where you and the others stand.'

'Sidharth Shah, Rishi Gaonkar and Avni Chadha. If the three of you are present, please come forward.'

Oh shit. I'm with Avni! What do I do now? What if I am unable to solve the equation? At least she knows now that I'm one of the top rank holders in class.

Avni and Rishi went and stood beside the professor, but Sidharth remained glued to his seat. It was only when his name was called out again that he stood up. As he passed Bani, she whispered, 'Are you really a topper? A back bencher who pays no heed to lectures?' Bani giggled. It only added to his nervousness.

He remembered a quote from Bill Gates and saw it as the perfect opportunity to use it. 'Bill Gates once said that if you want to pass, follow a first bencher but if you want to succeed in life, follow the last benchers.'

Sidharth wasn't sure the quote motivated Bani, but it sure made him feel good about himself. As he walked towards the professor, who was writing the equation on the blackboard, Avni saw him, and was completely baffled by his presence. *What is he doing here?* After their last encounter outside the liquor shop, she had hoped to stay away from him but God clearly had other plans. She avoided looking at him and turned towards Sonal, who had a big smile on her face.

I am sure he must have cheated in his examination. There's no way he could have been a topper otherwise. And anyway everyone will know the truth once he fails to solve the equation.

While Avni was finding it difficult to even stand next to him, Sidharth was on cloud nine. He could smell her fragrance and it made his body tingle. He couldn't gather the courage to look straight at her so he continued to look at the equation on the board. He just wanted the whole thing to get over soon so he could return to his seat and calm his nerves.

The professor was done writing the equation on the board three times and gave them five minutes to solve it.

All three of them took their respective places. Rishi took the centre position, easing some of Sidharth's nervousness. His mind had totally gone blank in Avni's presence. He took a deep breath and closed his eyes for a few seconds to regain his senses. Finally, he began solving the equation. After five minutes, all three were asked to set their chalks down.

'Well done, Sidharth and Rishi,' the professor exclaimed.

Is he being sarcastic or does he really mean it? Sidharth waited for the professor to continue.

'You both have solved it correctly,' he said and turning towards Avni added, 'You have made a slight mistake. Tally your equation with his,' he said pointing towards Sidharth's answer.

'The reason I told the toppers to solve it was this: Every year, I get at least one student who fails the engineering course. You may think that every third person in your neighbourhood is pursuing engineering but though that may be true, not every third person can excel in engineering. Your entrance and boards were different. Engineering won't be that easy. If, till now, you have been thinking that nothing could be worse than studying organic chemistry, then welcome to engineering.'

The professor asked the three students to go back to their places. Avni was very upset. What hurt her more was that she had lost out to Sidharth, of all people. Sonal sensed her feelings and tried to pacify her.

'Its okay. Things happen. But trust me, you are better than both of them.'

Avni was also disturbed about Sidharth being in the same class. She had wanted to stay away from her new neighbour, but now she would have to see his face each and every day in college. Just the thought of it made her feel disgusted.

Once the last lecture was over, Sidharth and Bani went to the canteen to eat something. As they walked, Bani said, 'I didn't think that I would befriend a topper on the first day. And such a good-looking topper at that.'

'Are you complimenting me or take a dig at me?' Sidharth smiled.

'No, I am really praising you. Though you don't have typical topper traits but you are good at heart.'

'See? Again.'

Bani laughed, not realizing she was constantly stereotyping the toppers. 'But I want a favour from you.' Sidharth looked at her in anticipation. 'I want you to help me in my studies. I am in engineering by chance and not choice. My parents forced me to take admission, else I would have never got into this shit. They think engineering and medical are the only two fields that exist.'

'Sure. I'll help you. But why did you choose mechanical? I mean girls generally go for computers or IT,' Sidharth inquired.

'My dad is a mechanical engineer,' Bani smirked.

'So you never wanted this stream?' Sidharth asked.

'Not really. But I love bikes, and I am very interested in their mechanism.'

'Oh nice. I have a sports bike,' Sidharth flaunted.

'Wow, drop me on the way somewhere please. Otherwise, I have to take a local train and its damn irritating.'

'Sure,' Sidharth agreed.

Sidharth and Bani had gotten along well on the first day itself, and Sidharth was happy that someone would notice and appreciate his sports bike.

Once classes were over for the day, Sidharth and Bani went to the car park, where he had parked his bike. Sidharth was delighted to show off his bike to Bani.

Meanwhile, Avni and Sonal had also made their way to the car park. Avni spotted Sidharth and her heart sank.

Not again! He really gets on my nerves.

'I think you both are destined to be together. If not you, then him and I both are destined for sure,' Sonal teased Avni.

'Now, don't go and start talking to him. I am too frustrated over the morning scene. So please. Or else I won't drop you home.'

'That's so rude. You're letting a stranger come in the way of our friendship,' Sonal continued to mock her.

Things got worse for Avni when she realized that her scooty was parked near Sidharth's bike. He would see her soon now; there was no escaping. Sidharth had his back towards her, and didn't seen her walking towards him. The moment she came and stood in front of him, his heart skipped a beat. Avni turned away and looked at her scooty. To her annoyance, she discovered that her tyre was punctured. She thought Sidharth was trying a filmi trick on her so that he could offer her a lift.

'Who do you think you are, Sidharth Shah? You think you can woo me by using these tricks? You think that by puncturing my bike, you will get an opportunity to drop me home? Listen mister, you better stay away from me. And I'll see to it that you pay for what you have done.'

Sonal tried to stop Avni but wasn't able to. Sidharth couldn't comprehend what Avni was talking about. He looked at her flat tyre. Before he could say anything to her, Bani came to his defence.

'Have you lost it? Grow up, girl. You aren't in school now. Did you see us do it? No, right? Then how can you blame us for it? Stop with your baseless allegations and just fuck off.'

Shit, this is going too far. Sidharth intervened. 'Stop it right here. Don't start with the abuses.' He pulled Bani back. He then looked at Avni and said, 'Avni, I haven't done it. That's all I can say to you.'

Avni didn't argue any further and walked away with Sonal, leaving Sidharth devasted. He had thought to reach out to her, now that they were in the same class, and now this had happened. It is said that love is a game of patience and hope, but his patience was fast running out.

Chapter 4

'So Mr Chadha, we've spoken about future opportunities and prospects, and how the matrimonial industry has evolved over the years. But there's one thing that I've been itching to ask you since the beginning of the interview,' said the reporter who had come to interview Balwinder and Mona at their office. 'It can be off record too if you're not comfortable with us printing it. So, as you know, the market is saturated with matrimonial websites, but I find that your working style is so different from other giants in the industry. How did you come up with the idea of Jodi.com?'

Balwinder laughed. 'You see, we've been in this industry for more than a decade now, and to be honest, before this idea struck us, I happened to meet a traditional matchmaker for my cousin. My wife and I were in a committed relationship for many years, and didn't need to take the matrimonial site route.'

'I have seen your videos on YouTube. You both are such an inspiration, even for the younger generation,' the reporter interjected. 'So about the making of Jodi. com . . .?'

'So ya, we were not sure how such websites operated, but we knew they essentially operated within certain tight-knit communities. Everybody knows everybody in those communities and so . . .'

Before he could finish, Balwinder's phone rang. It was Avni. He excused himself and went outside.

'Ya beta, how was your first day at college?'

'Dad, when are you both coming home? I have something urgent to discuss with you both.'

'I am in the middle of some work but I'll try and be home soon. Is everything fine?' he asked, concerned. She didn't sound like her regular jovial self.

'I have a flat tyre. Sonal is with me so we will first get it repaired and then head to the coaching centre to enrol ourselves for tuitions. Anyway, we'll talk more when I am home.' And with that, she disconnected the call. She wanted to ask them how Sidharth knew about their anniversary party and whether they had disclosed it to him, but since her dad was busy, she saved the question for later.

Balwinder disconnected the call and looked at a worried Mona, 'It was Avni. She said she wanted to talk about something.'

'It's nothing serious, right?'

'Doesn't seem so,' he replied, and went back in to continue with the interview.

'Ya, so it seemed awfully limiting that the choice of life partner was determined by how many people this person knew within the community. With the Internet being a global platform, you know, the point was to get like-minded people to connect, regardless of whether they belonged to a particular community or not. But the big players were already in the game so we realized we needed to be different.'

'So Jodi.com became the mediator, right?' she asked.

'Somewhat. But we were still in the experimenting phase.'

Mona interrupted him and asked the interviewer, 'Are you married?'

'Not yet,' the reporter blushed.

Mona smiled. 'So consider yourself in a situation where you have to find a match through a matrimonial site. You start looking for options and shortlist the best ones. But can you totally trust the information the other person has uploaded? And even if you take a step forward and meet the person, do you think he will tell you everything there is to know about him in all truthfulness? No, right?'

'Not in the first go for sure.'

'Then isn't it crazy or foolish to just trust a website blindly without a mediator in between?'

'I agree.'

Mona continued, 'And that's where we come in. Unlike other websites, we are not just connecting you online; for that you have dating apps like Bumble and Tinder. But matrimony is not the question of a blind date. It's one of the most important decisions of your life. And without a mediator to verify facts, how can you make that decision? And that's how we came up with the idea of Jodi.com. Our team personally meets both the guy and the girl before the first meeting can happen. There can be multiple meetings too to find out what each of them is looking for.'

The reporter was keenly listening to every word.

Balwinder took over from Mona. 'Being alone without any interfering parents around helps them open up to us more freely. We disclose all the details to the other party, who can then decide if they wish to go ahead with the meeting or not. If they don't like it, they can simply move on, rather than prolonging the situation. Obviously, this doesn't guarantee a 100 per cent safety net, but it's still something. Yes, it does add to our workload, but there's no gain without pain, right?'

'Brilliant. You guys are awesome. Thank you so much for your time,' said the reporter as she switched off her Dictaphone.

'It's our pleasure,' Balwinder said warmly.

Once the reporter left, Balwinder and Mona asked the staff to wrap up for the day, and left for home. On the way, they kept thinking about what Avni wanted to say to them. When they reached home, they saw Avni sitting on the sofa looking cross. She rushed to them as they entered the house.

'Did you guys meet our new neighbours by any chance?'

Avni's parents didn't see this coming.

'Why are you asking about them all of a sudden? Did they say something to you?'

'Please, just answer my question. Did you guys meet them or not?'

'Yes, we met the boy, Sidharth,' her mother replied.

'Ah, no wonder!' Avni sighed.

'Is something the matter?' Balwinder asked.

'I found out he's in the same college as me. Heck, not just the same college, we're in the same class! He knew about your anniversary party and when he mentioned it to me, I knew it had to be one of you who let the cat out of the bag. May I know what was the need to meet him all of a sudden?'

'So what's the big deal if he knows? We had gone out in the afternoon, and had given him a lift to the pharmacy since there was a problem with his bike.'

'Pharmacy? Are you sure?' Avni was certain she had seen him outside a liquor shop.

'We're certain. He told us he wanted to buy medicines for his nana.'

'What crap,' Avni responded. 'Neither is his bike broken nor was he buying medicines for his nana. I saw him buying liquor yesterday when I was out with Sonal. And he came to college on his perfectly okay bike today, so he is obviously lying about both things.'

Avni's father had a wide grin on his face.

'Why are you smiling?' Avni asked.

'Because now I understand why he was so nervous in the car. Had he told me he wanted to buy liquor, I would have guided him to a wine shop. What's there to hide?'

'Ya, and you would have told him to buy your favourite brand too, right?' His response infuriated Avni.

'You should see the positive side to this story. He is well mannered and courteous, and wanted to make a good impression on us.'

'You're unbelievable, Dad. Are you really defending his act? I don't want to talk to even you both.'

Avni walked out and went into her bedroom, banging the door shut behind her. As she lay on her bed, she tried to comprehend why the whole thing upset her so much. Was it because her parents had helped him or because he was proven superior in the class? Whatever it was, one thing was for sure—she absolutely and utterly disliked him.

~

Sometimes, the more the person you like ignores you, the more you start thinking about them. Sidharth didn't think he could like someone so much; but now that he did, he couldn't stop thinking about her. That night, he kept making trips to his balcony to catch a glimpse of her, but she didn't appear. Was she annoyed with him? He sure hoped not. He was finding it difficult to sleep. Maybe, if he could just see her once, his insomnia would finally loosen its tight grip on him. But she did not appear, and he finally fell asleep. The next morning, he got dressed before time and appeared at the breakfast table. Seeing him ready to leave early, his mother asked,

'Do you have an early lecture today? It's still 8:30 a.m. Weren't you supposed to leave at 9:30 a.m.?'

Nana was reading the newspaper in the living room and said in amusement, 'He's in college now. He must have promised some girl that he would come early.' He winked at Sidharth.

'Ya, you're right. I am waiting for someone to call, after which I'll leave,' he replied.

I too can play the game, Nanaji. His smile reflected his thought.

He ate his breakfast and retreated to his room.

Sidharth had spoken the truth to a certain extent. No one was going to call him but he was waiting for Avni to leave so that he could follow her and reach college at the same time as her. He wanted to have a word with her in private near the parking lot. He knew she wouldn't entertain him anywhere else, especially not in front of their classmates.

So, to keep a watch on Avni, he was standing in his balcony. He wasn't sure if what he felt for her was love, but he knew that he liked her and wanted to clear any misunderstanding between them. After a few minutes, he saw Avni leaving on her scooty and immediately rushed out of the house to follow her. He was careful not to bring his bike too close to her scooty for fear of being found out.

I am just going to tell her that whatever perception she has of me is false. She just happens to always catch me in the wrong place at the wrong time.

Avni finally reached the parking lot of the college. He would have liked to talk to her in private, but Sonal had been waiting for her, and went up to her as she parked. He was left with no choice.

He parked his bike quickly and went up to her. 'Avni, I want to talk to you.'

Avni took one look at him and started walking briskly. She was trying her best to ignore him.

'There's been a misunderstanding . . .'

But before he could complete his sentence, she had already walked off. He didn't chase her, thinking that would make the situation worse, and stood there in disappointment. All of sudden, he felt a hand on his shoulders. He turned to see a group of half a dozen burly-looking boys staring at him. They were wearing black leather jackets which had 'The Big Bikers' written over them. The leader of the pack was wearing biker gloves and a bandana around his head.

'So, the bike outside is his?' the leader asked his gang.

'Yes, DK,' they replied in unison.

'Any problem?' Sidharth asked trying to put up a brave front.

'Do you think you can just come to college on your Karizma sports bike and try and act all cool in front of the girls?'

Sidharth thought they were referring to Avni. 'No, it was just misunderstanding. We are both neighbours.'

'To hell with her,' DK replied dismissively. Sidharth realized he wasn't talking about her. 'We are

"The Big Bikers" and if you want to brag about your bike in this college, you have to be part of our gang.'

'But why?' Sidharth asked politely.

'You can't ask any stupid questions. You just have to do as I say.' DK's arrogance reflected in his tone.

Sidharth thought for a few seconds. *What's the harm in being part of their gang?* He was seeking validation; he wanted everyone to notice him, and this was the perfect way to do that.

'But getting into the club isn't so easy,' said DK and added, 'You need to do a couple of things first. So you're in mechanical first year?'

'Yes. And you too? But you don't look like a fresher,' Sidharth commented, looking at DK's appearance.

'DK doesn't clear any subject till he has mastered it. That's why he is repeating the first year,' said one of DK's gang members.

The gang members laughed, and DK gave Sidharth a friendly punch. *Oh great, they do have a sense of humour,* Sidharth thought. *Maybe they aren't as scary as they seem.* 'So what am I supposed to do?' asked Sidharth.

'You have to enrol yourself for the "head of the Mechanical Student Committee" post. The entire class votes and appoints the head. If you become the head of the committee, you will help us with our attendance since we hardly attend any lectures. And secondly, you have to win a race against any of the guys in the group.

We race on the road right behind college once the day's lectures are over.'

'Will I get the same jacket as you if I win?' He had been marvelling at their attire since they appeared on the scene.

This question made even DK break into a smile. Sidharth won the race later in the day, impressing the other members in the gang. He was glad to have met like-minded people and they spent the rest of the day talking about bikes, riding clubs, their favourite riders and so on. At the end of the day, The Big Bikers gave him a jacket similar to theirs, much to his delight. He was officially inducted in their club now!

~

A couple of days later, a professor announced that the 'Mechanical Students Committee' selection for different posts would commence shortly. He addressed the entire class.

'All those students who wish to enrol their names for the head committee selection, kindly meet me during the break. The shortlisted students will need to address the class in the second half today and the rest of the students will vote for them.'

Sidharth was the first to enrol himself; he would have done it even without DK's suggestion. There were around fifteen students who had enrolled during the break, and ten positions were up for grabs—one position for the head of the committee and the rest for honorary members. Avni had enrolled herself too but didn't know Sidharth was in the running. When Sonal found out, she rushed to tell Avni before the break ended.

'Do you know who are the other students competing with you?'

'I know only a couple of guys who had come with me to the professor's cabin to enrol their names. I don't know the rest,' Avni replied.

'Even I don't know the names of all fifteen but I know one name that will be of interest to you.'

Avni knew who Sonal was referring to. 'Don't tell me!'

Sonal nodded and said teasingly, 'Yes. Your best friend Sidharth Shah.'

Avni turned around to look at Sidharth who was busy chatting with members of the biking gang she had seen outside class earlier. Unbeknown to her, they had come especially to vote for him. She looked at Sidharth and the gang, and knew something was cooking between them.

'Do you think this guy who's a complete ass and friends with these biker thugs deserves to be part of the committee?' asked Avni.

'I don't know. I find him cute.'

Avni didn't want to give the matter any further attention. She was focused on winning. She remembered her life mantra, which she had framed on her wall, 'Always be competitive.' No matter how much she tried to avoid Sidharth, she knew there was no escaping him, not for the next few years of engineering at least.

Once the break was over, the class-in-charge entered with the list of students in his hand. He called out their names one by one. Each candidate took to the podium to give impassioned speeches on why they deserved to be part of the committee. Sidharth was listening to their speeches, thinking what could he say differently that would make everyone vote for him. He didn't know he was up against Avni here too. When Avni's name was announced, it caught him completely off guard. Staring at her, Sidharth forgot about everything else. It was like nothing else mattered to him, neither the selections, nor the lectures, nothing.

Avni introduced herself and started addressing the students.

'It's said that women make better leaders because of their traits of compassion and empathy and I couldn't agree more. With only a handful of girls in this class, I urge you to vote for a candidate who will listen to your problems without any kind of judgement. A yes for me is a yes to a better you. And together it's is a yes to a better life in this college.'

Avni had used the feminine card to her advantage. Sidharth was completely floored by her speech.

What kind of an idiot wouldn't vote for a girl like that? She can have my vote, he thought, completely forgetting that he was competing with her.

He totally blanked out when his name was called out. He had thankfully made notes on a sheet of paper. He took to the stage and unfolded the paper. But as he looked at the students staring at him, something overcame him and he discarded the paper.

'You might be asking yourself, 'Should Sidharth really be the student body president? Toppers don't generally fare well with the rest of the students. But I am not one of those toppers who are always glued to their first bench and may as well take it home as a momento after graduation.' His comment made the students break into a laugh. 'I won't give a long boring speech, but trust me, a "last bencher" leader is always better than a "first bencher", if you know what I mean.'

His speech met with thunderous applause. After the votes were cast, the results were announced in an hour. While Sidharth was elected the head, Avni became a member of the committee. When his name was called out, even he was flabbergasted. After Avni's speech, he thought he barely had a chance, but he had hit the right chord with the students. Who wouldn't want a back-bencher leader who will allow the rest to mass bunk rather than complaining to the faculty? DK and his gang came forward to congratulate Sidharth but Avni was furious. She had been the best in everything so far, be it in school or junior college. Until the arrival of Sidharth Shah in her life.

~

A week after the committee selection, Avni still held a deep grudge against Sidharth. For the whole week, they attended the lectures in the same classroom and even attended the committee meetings together, but Avni didn't speak a word to him and always maintained a safe distance.

Sonal knew she had to put an end to this tension between them. 'You should get over it. I agree your speech was brilliant, but maybe on that day he was slightly better than you. Why can't you just accept it and move on?'

'I have accepted it. Why are you digging up the same topic over and over again?' Avni asked.

'You may be over the selection. But you are certainly not over Sidharth.'

'So, you think he's better than me, do you? Why don't you join the gang that he roams with and spend your dad's hard-earned money on those reckless bike stunts?' Avni irritation was palpable.

Sidharth and Bani both had started spending all their free time with DK and his gang on the campus. Seeing them together irked Avni more. She hated guys who weren't focused in life, and behaved like vagrant morons.

Bani was pleading with Sidharth to bunk the upcoming practicals. 'That day you were quoting Bill Gates and now you're not ready to bunk one practical. Do you think he became the person he is by attending lectures? He was a drop out.'

'He was a Harvard drop out. And I am not even in IIT. So don't give me such lame examples.'

'What yaar, don't be such a spoilsport. We can attend all the lectures from tomorrow. I promise we'll not even bunk one lecture.'

'Ya, and that tomorrow never comes.'

It was the first workshop of the semester and he didn't want to miss it. He forced Bani to attend it with him, and they made their way to the workshop lab. All the students of the M2 batch already gathered inside, including the professor. Avni was in M1 and had a different practical session. Sonal was in M2.

'Three students on one table,' instructed the professor.

Sonal joined Sidharth at the table while Bani was allotted another. The professor showed the entire batch a demo of the job and asked each batch to perform the demo with the help of the job sheet kept on the table.

'So you always wanted to do engineering?' Sidharth asked Sonal.

'Yes and no.'

'What does that mean?'

'I mean, if not for engineering, I wouldn't know what to do. And as Avni was taking the engineering entrance exam, so did I.'

Sidharth laughed at her reply. It was Sonal's turn to ask, 'So, you've shifted to Mumbai recently, no? You should have come to Mumbai a few days prior to college so you could have got used to Mumbai's lifestyle.'

'Places are the same everywhere. It's the people who matter. And the people here are quite rude as per my observance. In contrast, Gujaratis are such a sweet and friendly lot. And I'm not being partial,' Sidharth replied.

Sonal was prompt to contradict his view. 'You couldn't be more wrong. Mumbaikars are warm and friendly too. You just have to give the city some time.'

'I know but I haven't liked any of the interactions so far,' he said in a veiled reference to Avni.

'I know who you are talking about,' Sonal smiled, and said, 'It's not her fault. She feels you are a reckless alcoholic.'

'Wow. That's quite a title. I am sure by the end of engineering she will leave no adjectives unused,' Sidharth smirked.

Sonal looked down, slightly embarrassed for being blunt. 'Sorry if you felt bad, but I just wanted to be honest with you. And you don't seem bad at all to me.'

'Thank you for saying that. I am sure you wouldn't have even talked to me if she was here.'

'It's not like that. It's just that she has a perception and . . .'

Sidharth interrupted Sonal. 'That day when you guys saw me, I was buying liquor for my nana. And I didn't puncture her scooty. I mean, why would I? She thought I was looking for an opportunity to give her a ride back home on my bike? I mean, is there a 'C' written on my forehead?'

Sonal was convinced with his explanation. 'To be honest, on both the occasions, I have taken your side.'

'Is this how girls flirt?' Sidharth winked, and they both started giggling.

Sidharth felt relieved knowing that at least Avni's friend didn't make him out to be a devil. They chatted some more and didn't realize when Bani came and stood behind them.

'God, Bani, you scared me! For a split second, I thought the professor was overhearing us.'

'So all the grudges are over between you both?'

'There weren't any in the first place,' Sonal was quick to add.

'Anyway, tomorrow is our fresher's party and I want to know how excited you guys are?' asked Bani.

'Damn excited,' Sonal said enthusiastically.

'Me too. No more boring lectures!' Bani said giving a high-five to Sidharth.

He suddenly remembered that he had to go for a meeting organized by the student committee. He excused himself and headed out.

'See you both tomorrow at the party.'

~

A life in engineering is made up of three primary stages:

1. Fresher's party
2. What the fuck is happening?
3. Farewell party

The students of DC College of Engineering were about to witness the first stage. The students had left no stone unturned to make it a gala event. Sidharth, being the head of the committee, was garnering all the attention, while the committee members including Avni were made to carry out all the arrangements. The whole thing was testing Avni's patience but she tried her best to keep calm and carry on. She was dressed in a stunning black dress and Sidharth couldn't take his eyes off her.

The first surprise of the evening was the mob dance of which Sidharth and The Big Bikers were a part. It was a three-minute performance, and was met with loud hoots and cheers by the onlookers. The dance was followed by some stand-up comedy and a few skits. Once the stage performances began, Sidharth, Bani and the gang settled down in one corner. DK observed Sidharth staring at Avni who was chatting with Sonal and some other girls in one corner.

'You like her. Don't you?' he asked turning towards Sidharth.

'No . . . Just that she is . . .'

DK didn't allow him to explain. 'Ya, I know she is your neighbour. But you are not her bodyguard. So why do you keep staring at her?' he teased.

The rest of the gang members joined in and started pulling his leg. They insisted he go talk to her and tell her how he felt.

'No way! I am not going to fall in your trap,' Sidharth replied.

'Should I go speak to her for you?' asked Bani. 'I'll tell her that even though she hates Sidharth, he's in loooove with her.'

'Shut up, you ass,' Sidharth rebuked.

DK and his gang felt the only way Sidharth would loosen up was if he had a bit of alcohol. They handed him a cup of vodka mixed with coke without telling him, and Sidharth gulped it in one go. By the time he realized his drink had been spiked, it was too late.

'Did you mix alcohol in my drink?' he asked feeling a little tipsy.

'A little,' Bani replied. 'Doesn't it taste so much better now?' She gave her glass to DK for a refill.

Sidharth saw his gang was having a good time and he didn't want to ruin it for them, so he drank along. He gulped down his sixth drink and threw the Thermocol glass on the floor. 'That's it, I'm done,' he exclaimed.

'Enough of drinking. Let's dance,' DK suggested and ran towards the dance floor. The stage was full of people but their gang managed to push everyone aside and reach the centre. Even in his inebriated state, Sidharth was looking for Avni. He saw her standing near the dance floor looking uneasy. Some of the guys were forcing her to join them, making her feel uncomfortable. Sidharth could tell things would get ugly so he went closer to Avni and pulled her on the dance floor, away from the unruly looking boys. Avni was taken aback by Sidharth's action.

What the fuck? Has he gone crazy? Bani thought to herself. She knew he was high and didn't know what he was doing. Even DK and the gang were surprised.

Avni was still in a state of shock and the discomfort reflected in her body language. Sidharth placed his hand on her back and pulled her closer. She tried to free herself but he had a strong grip on her. When he wouldn't let go, she gave him a hard slap on the face, much to everyone's shock. Someone asked the DJ to stop the music.

A sudden silence filled the air. Avni felt humiliated and left the dance floor in tears. Sonal followed her out to console her. Sidharth could still feel the echo of the slap. He felt embarrassed and miserable for what had he done.

Chapter 5

Sometimes life throws things at you that are way beyond your control. Sidharth chose to stay silent and not react to Avni's slap. He knew he was equally at fault. But he had to face the heat from the head of the department who had asked him to bring his parents to college the next day or else he would get suspended.

When he reached home, he barely interacted with anyone and went straight to his room and locked himself in. He wanted to spend some time just by himself and his thoughts. He felt anxious thinking Avni would never talk to him again and that it was perhaps over before it could even begin. Adding to his anxiety was the fact that he had to tell his mother about what had happened. He didn't know how to bring it up and called Bani for advice.

'My mom will kick me out of the house if she finds out what happened,' Sidharth said.

Bani tried to calm him down with an idea. 'Dude, do not tell your mom anything. I know someone who can come to college as your fake dad. He had acted as my fake dad in the twelfth standard when my parents were hauled up for my low attendance. No one will come to know, trust me. We can pay him with bottles of his favourite alcohol.'

'That's asking for more trouble. If I get caught, I'll get screwed,' Sidharth replied. He wasn't too enthused about the idea. 'I shouldn't have got drunk. It's all your fault. You pushed me to keep drinking. And I lost control.'

'Yes, and I also pushed you to dance with Avni without her permission, right?' Bani replied.

'Anyway, I think I have no choice.'

Sidharth hung up and stepped outside his bedroom. His grandfather was watching a reporter screaming on the top of his lungs on a prime time news show, unaware that Sidharth had some breaking news of his own.

'Mom, I need to talk to you.'

'I am busy right now, can't you see?' his mom said as she kneaded the dough for dinner.

But Sidharth pleaded with her and she finally stepped out of the kitchen, washing her hands in the basin on her way out. Nana knew something was up, and switched off the TV. As she stepped closer, his mother finally saw the bruises on his face. She panicked and rushed towards him.

'What happened? Is everything okay?' she asked worriedly.

Nana walked towards him to inspect the bruises more closely. 'Did something happen in college?'

Sidharth didn't know what to tell them. He looked down, unable to make eye contact. He knew what would follow but somehow he gathered courage and spoke up.

'Mom, the thing is that today in college . . . we had a freshers' party and . . .'

'Come straight to the point. Did you pick up a fight with someone?'

How should I tell her? If I tell her about Avni, she'll take an avatar of Kali Ma. I better stick to the fight. 'Actually, I got into a fight with some seniors, and the professors saw it. They've called you to college tomorrow to meet the HOD.'

I want to tell her the entire episode. Why am I focusing on just the fight that happened after the party? If she comes to know about Avni tomorrow, she'll be even angrier. No . . . I can't tell her. I'll think of a more plausible explanation tonight.

His mom was devastated. He was half expecting her to slap him blue in the face, but she just stood in her place looking zapped. Sidharth could see tears in her eyes. He looked at Nana, who was his usual cool self.

'Mom, I am sorry.' He thought of telling her the whole story but just couldn't find the courage to do so.

His mother finally spoke up. 'Didn't I tell you that you have responsibilities? Do you know the amount of effort we are making so that you can get the best education? And how are you repaying us for it? It's hardly been a few days since college started, and look at you! These years will decide the course of your life.'

Damn, why are all parents as dramatic as a Sooraj Bharjatiya movie?

The dramatic scene finally came to an end when his mom retired to her room. Meanwhile, Avni was getting it from Sonal. Sonal had called up Bani just when Sidharth had disconnected Bani's call, and learnt about the entire episode.

'I know what he did was wrong but his intention wasn't. Even I felt the seniors were trying to touch you inappropriately. I should have said something then, but then I thought I was overthinking and ignored it all. But now after speaking with Bani, I feel like I was right.'

'I don't believe you. You are just taking his side because you were partners in the workshop session.'

'Exactly, and that's the reason I know that he isn't as bad as you think he is. Do you even know that after we left, he was bashed up by the professors and when he was about to leave the campus, the same seniors got hold of him and started beating him badly?'

'Oh please, why would they do so? It's another one of his lies,' Avni replied.

'Because when they got into a fight, one of the seniors told him that he likes you and when Sidharth didn't let him hit on you, he got offended. They were drunk and were trying to take advantage of the huge crowd. If DK and his gang wouldn't have come to Sidharth's rescue the matter would have got worse. But our HOD saw them before they could escape and warned them that he would suspend each and every one of them if they didn't bring their parents to college tomorrow. The other guys didn't seem to care but Sidharth was visibly upset.'

Avni did feel slightly bad upon hearing about the suspension, but she was still hung up on what had happened.

'I don't understand why you feel that I am in the wrong here.'

'I am saying again that what he did was wrong, but the way you slapped him was not right either. I feel you should apologize to him.'

'I am not going to do that at any cost,' Avni responded, and disconnected the call.

All through the night, Avni kept tossing and turning, brooding over what Sonal had told her. She could hardly catch any sleep. Had she really acted irrationally? Should she be the bigger person here and apologize? She couldn't come to a conclusion. The next morning, she went to Nani's place in the same confused state of mind. Whenever she found herself at a crossroads, she would turn to Nani for advice.

Once she reached her house, she told her everything in detail.

'You are just exaggerating things. Did he ever talk rudely with you or misbehave with you in any way?'

'No. Not before yesterday's event. But how could he do what he did?' Avni asked.

'I can understand you're hurt by what he did and in the heat of the moment, you reacted that way. But if what Sonal is saying is true, he actually wanted to protect you from those boys. Wouldn't you have reacted similarly if you saw something like this happen?'

Avni didn't know what to say. She knew her nani was right.

'Also, he is your classmate, your new neighbour, and like you said, he seems brilliant in studies too. But you're continuing to focus on his flaws. Don't forget, there are flaws in every person, and at your age, everyone's allowed to be a little reckless.'

Avni nodded. 'Do you think I should apologize? I'll do it if you ask me to.'

Her nani smiled and said, 'Don't do it for my sake. Do it if you truly want to. And what do you have to lose if you apologize?'

Avni didn't want to disagree with Nani. But if she apologized, she wanted him to do it too. She wasn't too thrilled by Nani's advice, but after their brief conversation, she had made up her mind. After some more time with her, she left for the college. As she made her way towards the lecture hall with Sonal, she asked her, 'Do you have Sidharth's number?'

Sonal was taken by surprise. 'Now please don't stretch the topic. We've already spoken too much on this and I don't want . . .'

Avni interrupted her. 'I just want to apologize to him. I think you were right.'

Sonal couldn't believe her ears. 'What did you just say? You want to apologize to Sidharth? Are you sure?'

Avni saw the smile on her face. 'There's no need to get excited. I've been thinking and I feel it was wrong of me to slap him. That's it.'

'What did you eat this morning? I think you should include that in your regular diet,' Sonal teased her and fished out her phone from the pocket. She didn't have Sidharth's number but called Bani, who told her they were outside the HOD's cabin. Sonal and Avni rushed to the cabin.

By the time they reached, Sidharth was stepping out of the cabin with his mom. His heart skipped a beat on seeing Avni standing outside. Somewhere he was feeling guilty, even though his heart was jumping to the tune of a thousand beats. His mother wasn't too pleased on seeing Avni and the other girls. She walked right past them and made her way towards the lift. Sidharth wanted to stop and talk with them—he could tell they were waiting outside for a word with him. But seeing his mother walk off, he couldn't do much.

Shit man, why do mothers have to act like the world is collapsing at every little thing? Why do they make a big deal about everything?

As Sidharth hailed an auto for his mother outside the college gate, she gave him a stern warning.

'This is the first and the last time I am sparing you. I don't want to hear any more complaints related to that girl or anyone else henceforth.'

'Okay, Mom. Now, bye. I am getting late for my lecture.'

Saying so, Sidharth rushed in, and saw the girls standing outside the classroom. Nervously, he took a few steps in their direction. Avni too took a step closer to him and said:

'I am sorry. I think I shouldn't have hit you.'

She noticed the slight bruises on his face and recollected Sonal telling her about the fight. Sidharth felt an adrenaline rush. It was the first time Avni was talking to him directly and in such close proximity. Internally, he was battling between what to say and what not to.

He was having trouble getting words out of his mouth. 'Why are you apologizing? I should be sorry. It was inappropriate on my part to just touch you without your permission. It won't happen again, I promise.'

'It's okay,' Avni replied with a slight smile on her face, and all of them entered the class.

Their short interaction left him feeling nervous and excited in equal parts. He loved even her half-hearted smile. He didn't know what to say to her; all he knew was he wanted to spend more time with her. He wanted to ask her for her phone number but didn't want to seem too eager. He decided to take her number from Sonal instead. Once he saved her number, he opened her contact on WhatsApp and kept staring at her DP.

Damn, she looks so beautiful here! If only I could be with her for eternity. If only I could look into her eyes, touch her once, feel her close to me.

Once home, he kept thinking about texting her the whole day but couldn't find the courage. Instead, he kept gazing at her DP.

Eventually, after dinner, he retreated to his bedroom and began to type a message to her.

Hi, Avni. Sidharth this side. Thanks for forgiving me and for being the first one to initiate the talk. You know the first time I saw you in your car, I had butterflies in my stomach. I was not a believer in love at first sight. Not until I met you. I just want to tell you that I haven't met anyone as beautiful as you. You are different from the other girls. You are simple, sweet and innocent. And that's what I love most about you. Can we be friends?

He kept staring at the message. Just as we was about to press the send button, he had a change of mind.

'*Hi Avni, Sidharth this side. Thanks for forgiving me. Friends?*'

His heart began to pound the moment he saw the tick turn blue.

After a few minutes, his phone beeped. He opened his WhatsApp to see a message from Avni.

Avni: ☺

Does it mean that she is OK being friends with me? Are we friends now? Why couldn't she say anything more? What does a smiley mean? Why can't she be a little more expressive? Damn, understanding girls is more difficult that learning coding.

He wanted to text her again but didn't want to seem too desperate. He hoped that she would text him again. He kept his mobile next to his pillow and slept, dreaming of her.

～

Being in love is the most beautiful feeling in the world and Sidharth was in love! He looked forward to college as he would get to interact with Avni. His body felt like an internal-combustion engine. There was a continuous combustion of thoughts and desires inside him that generated a huge amount of frustration with college life. Avni acted as a coolant for him and made the lectures interesting.

For the first month of college, Avni was reluctant to interact with him, and hesitated to be around him, preferring instead to head back home after college hours. By the third month, she had become good friends with Sidharth, but it was only friendship and nothing more than that. With time, Sidharth too started to feel more comfortable being around Avni. They began leaving for college together on their respective vehicles at the same time and even returned together on most days. Sometimes, the owner of the grocery store would tease him about his growing closeness to Avni.

'You seem to be getting too friendly with Chadha's daughter. Boy, you are running faster than the Rajdhani. What's cooking?'

'We're just friends. And how does it concern you? Please stay out of my personal matters or I will have to report you,' Sidharth said with a stern expression.

'Don't get furious. I am just kidding. If you guys are happy, then great, who am I to say anything?'

In all these months, he had not told a single person about his feelings for Avni. But Bani and Sonal could tell something was up by the way he acted around her. Sidharth, Avni, Sonal and Bani were their own little gang by now. It was report submission day and all the students had gathered outside the staffroom with files in their hands.

'Bro, I am fucking scared. I am sure our class-in-charge will throw the submission files at my face seeing how low my attendance is,' Bani exclaimed.

'Too late now. I've been telling you to attend lectures to ensure the minimum attendance at least. But you don't listen. Now face the music,' Sidharth replied and turned to Avni. 'How much is yours? I am sure you're topping in the attendance department too.'

Avni smiled and said, 'Mine is 82 per cent, but I'm still nervous.'

Sonal joined in. 'As am I. I hope everything goes well.'

Sidharth laughed and said, 'If you both are feeling anxiety after having an attendance of 82 per cent and 78 per cent, then I think Bani should be dead by now. Hers is not even 50 per cent.'

'You are in a mood to do a stand-up comedy now?' Bani said with a serious expression on her face.

'Don't worry. My attendance is below 60 per cent. If you make it, I will too,' Sidharth said trying to sound cool.

'You will get extra concession, being part of the student committee. I get fucking no concession.' Bani's apprehension was visible on her face.

Avni looked at Sidharth and said, 'If you would have spent more time with us than with those biker idiots, you would not have kept your hopes on her. You should always be competitive.'

Sonal intervened. 'You and your fundas! Don't you get irritated by them?'

Sidharth wasn't listening to Sonal.

More time with us? Does she mean she wants to spend more time with me? Has she started liking me too?

Even after being good friends with her for so many months, when it came to expressing his feelings for Avni, he talked more in his head than out in the open. He had given her enough subtle hints that he liked her, but she never once reciprocated. He wanted to tell her that he would love to spend all his time with her. He wanted to tell her how much he loved her. But all he did was tease her like Sonal.

'I am sure Avni hasn't even skipped a traffic light once in her life,' Sidharth joked. Avni frowned at his comment while he continued, 'Our college years will never come back, so we should enjoy and make the most of every moment. Make memories. Remember what Bill Gates said . . .'

'Enough with your Bill Gates. I am sure even he must not have quoted that dialogue as much as you,' teased Bani.

Avni thought for a moment before saying, 'I don't completely disagree with your statement. But if you don't achieve what you set out to in life, you will never want to relive these memories.'

Does she want me to achieve something in life? Does she want to relive our memories together? I can't take these cryptic messages any more. I have to tell her how I feel about her.

Bani suggested that if the submissions went well, they should celebrate. 'Let's spend an entire day together; we can watch a movie, have some pizza and have a good time. We haven't really gone out this entire semester, you know, except for the occasional chaat.'

Sidharth and Sonal loved the idea but Avni put a dampener on their plans. 'No, you guys carry on. I have to study. Exams are just around the corner.'

Avni wasn't the kind of girl who enjoyed going on outings. She preferred to stay focused on her studies and use her time wisely, especially when exams were approaching.

The submissions went off smoothly. But Sidharth couldn't decipher the complications that spun around in his head. Their outing did not materialise, but Sidharth's plan to propose to Avni was still on. He could no longer keep his feelings to himself. But did Avni feel the same way for Sidharth?

Chapter 6

'*See you at 6 p.m. Sonal and Bani will also be here by then. And bring the maths notes I had given you,*' Avni texted Sidharth.

He smiled on seeing the notification from her. They had decided to sit for group studies at Avni's house. It had been a few days since the submission, but Sidharth was still not able to express his feelings to Avni. This added anxiety didn't let him concentrate on his studies either.

He called up Bani before the meeting. 'Hi, you are coming at 6, right? To Avni's place?'

'Ya obviously. Why are you asking such a stupid question?'

'I called you to talk about something else. But you don't seem very interested in hearing me out, so let's leave it.'

'Did you just wake up or something? You sound too serious.'

'Actually, the thing is . . . I don't know how to tell you.'

'Why don't you become a daily soap scriptwriter? You are so good at stretching scenes unnecessarily.'

'I am serious . . . Okay, so here goes. I think I'm in love with Avni.'

Bani wasn't surprised at this revelation. 'Are you really serious about her or is it just a fleeting emotion?' she asked.

'I am serious about her. I really do love her a lot. I've tried my best to keep my feelings in check but I just can't now. Every time I hear a romantic song, I can only visualise her in my head. But please don't tell anyone about my feelings for her. Not even Sonal.'

Bani could tell he was smitten with Avni. 'I trust you. But I don't know if she will reciprocate your love, honestly. She's too focused on her studies to pay you any attention. Do you think she loves you back? Because I haven't seen her express it so far.'

'I think so,' Sidharth said hesitatingly.

'So anyway, we are meeting in the evening at her house to study, right? Maybe you can reveal your feelings to her then? Or at least give her a slight hint so you can find out exactly how she feels.'

Sidharth liked the idea but he was too scared of the consequences. He feared Avni would stop talking to him altogether. He googled ways to express love to a girl but couldn't find a video worth trying. He was an ordinary guy, not some Raj, Rahul or Raichand from a Karan Johar movie. In spite of all the odds stacked against him, he decided to go ahead with his plan. At sharp 6 p.m., he saw Sonal from his balcony. She waited for him to come down and when he reached, she gave him a huge smile. Sidharth couldn't understand what she was trying to convey.

'What? Why are you giving me that look?'

'I heard you're stepping onto a battlefield today.'

I am going to kill Bani. I had told her not to tell anyone.

'Did Bani say something to you?'

'Of course. She did. When did this happen?' Sonal asked inquisitively. She wanted to know more from him.

Sidharth didn't want to go into any more detail. 'It's a long story. I'll tell you some other day. But please don't say a word to Avni or anyone else. Not you at least.'

'Don't worry, I won't say anything,' Sonal said and started walking towards Avni's house. 'But I must say you're brave to enter the battlefield without any armour.'

'Don't make me more nervous than I already am.'

'That's the whole fun of it,' Sonal winked.

By the time they reached Avni's gate, Bani had also reached. Sidharth shot her an infuriated look. She gestured to Sidharth and said apologetically, 'Don't worry, Sonal is one of us now. We can trust her.' They rang Avni's doorbell.

Sidharth had been to her house briefly a couple of times before to exchange notes but never for an extended study hour. Avni's dad opened the door and welcomed everyone inside. Sidharth sat on the sofa in the living room and looked around. The main wall of the living room had a huge portrait of Guru Nanak Devji.

'Avni is in Babaji's room with her mother. She'll be here in a few minutes,' he said.

The girls were trying their best to conceal their giggles. Sidharth frowned at them. A few minutes later, Avni joined them. She introduced her friends to her mother.

Avni's mom instantly recognized Sidharth. 'How are you, Beta?'

'I am fine, Aunty. How are you doing?' Sidharth smiled.

'All good. And how's your nana? I hope he's taking his medicines on time?' she teased.

Sidharth coughed to hide his awkwardness. Avni excused them and led the three to her bedroom. Sidharth was excited and nervous at the same time. In his dreams he would have wanted to be alone with Avni in her room. But his reality was far from it. He still felt a rush of adrenaline as he stepped inside.

'My parents know you were at the liquor shop and not the pharmacy on the day they gave you a lift,' Avni said as she bolted the door to her room.

Sidharth was dumbstruck upon hearing this. And all this time he thought he had successfully tricked them.

'Damn, now how do I make you believe that I don't drink?' Sidharth suddenly remembered dragging her to the dance floor after a couple of drinks and the slap that landed on his face after. He decided to swiftly change the topic. 'Anyway, should we focus on maths now? That's what we are here for, right?'

'We are. We can't say that about you, Bani replied. She left no opportunity to irritate Sidharth.

'Ignore her. She is an idiot,' said Sidharth to a confused-looking Avni who didn't know what Bani meant. They opened Kambojkar's maths textbook.

Bani, who hadn't even brought the textbook with her, said, 'If I happen to meet this Kambojkar guy or anyone from his family one day, I'm going to ask him what fun he has by torturing students.'

'Why don't we study from Easy Solutions? The entire paper will be based on questions from the last five years,' chipped in Sonal.

'But you still need to know the basics to solve those questions, right? Avni asked.

'Exactly,' Sidharth nodded in agreement with Avni.

'Guys, you both are toppers. We are more than happy if we get even forty marks.'

Not willing to leave anything to fate, the two class toppers forced Bani and Sonal to study. They continued studying for the next couple of hours. When they finally took a break and Sidharth checked his mobile phone, he saw a couple of missed calls from his mom. She wasn't too kicked about her son going over to Avni's to study for obvious reasons. She had even left him a message on his phone.

'Why is your phone on silent mode? I've been calling you for the last thirty minutes. Anyway, by what time are you coming home? Or do you plan on having dinner there as well?'

He could sense the sarcasm in her message. He replied saying he would be back in time for dinner. Avni excused herself to go to the washroom, and that's when Sidharth's eyes fell on the many quotes framing her wall.

'Never get too attached to someone.'

Does she really mean it? He had come mentally prepared to divulge his feelings to her but when he read the quote, he wasn't sure if he should go ahead with the plan. Sonal told him the wall frames were a gift from her grandmother, and that Avni really believed in them. There was also a collage of pictures of Avni with her nani near her study table. When Avni returned, she saw him studying the collage with intensity.

'You're very close to your Nani, right?

'Yes. She is my lifeline,' Avni replied.

Just the mere mention of her made Avni emotional. Sidharth realized it wasn't a good time to tell her how he felt. Afraid of rejection, he dropped the plan. Just then, they heard voices from the living room.

'Don't look outside; they'll kill you in one shot.'

'Follow me, change the location, or else he'll throw a grenade.'

'What the fuck is happening outside?' asked a terrified Sonal.

'It's just my parents playing PUBG. Ignore them,' replied Avni. It was a normal thing in her house these days. 'The game has driven them crazy. They live stream it on their YouTube channel.'

'You are blessed to have such parents. They must be so much fun to be around,' Sidharth chimed in.

'Only I know what I have to go through,' Avni replied.

Sidharth wanted to join them in the game. It would also help divert him from thoughts of professing his love to Avni.

'Why don't you guys continue studying and I'll join you in a while.' He stepped out into the living room. Her parents weren't live streaming the game but playing on their mobile phones.

'How many kills by now?' Sidharth asked taking a step closer to them.

'Don't ask. Only thirty-five are alive and I have got just two kills.'

'Be specific. Two bot kills.' Avni's mother laughed.

'Bots are the saviours. My entire squad leaves everything aside and runs behind one bot to assure one kill.'

Avni's dad looked up from his game and asked, 'You play PUBG too?'

'I am on the Diamond tier. Why don't we play together after this game ends?' Sidharth suggested.

'What's your K/D?' Avni's dad asked.

'2.2.'

'Oh, we have a pro in the house.'

They played the next game with Sidharth, and the hours flew by. Soon, it was dark, and Sidharth realized he better head home before dinner time or else he would invite the wrath of his mother. His plan to say something to Avni had failed miserably. Avni, on the other hand, was irritated seeing him waste away his study time playing games and still getting good grades in his exams.

What a wasted opportunity, Sidharth thought as he entered home sulking. It was the first time he was so madly in love with someone. It was the first time he wanted to hold someone's hand; feel her touch, hug her and kiss her.

Sidharth and Avni . . . will these names ever be taken in the same breath? He thought about her all through dinner, and until he went to sleep.

~

Sidharth, without saying anything, had spoken to Avni in hundred silent ways. At times, you love a person so much but can't tell them because you don't want to lose them. You don't want things to be awkward if they don't feel the same way. So, you love them in silence, you miss them in silence, you think about them silently and pretend like you are absolutely fine with it. But sometimes, silent love hurts. And Sidharth wasn't able to take the pain that came along with suppressing his feelings. His exams commenced, but Sidharth's attention was elsewhere.

Nana had observed the uneasiness in his body language, and a night before his second exam paper, he decided to find out what the matter was.

'Sidharth, are you alright? Is there anything your old nana can help you with?'

Sidharth didn't want to tell him what was troubling him. 'Just the exam pressure, Nana. That's all,' he lied.

'Are you sure there's nothing else? Because I've never seen you this lost. You know you can tell me anything, right?'

Sidharth couldn't hold back any longer. He told his grandfather everything—how he had fallen for Avni the day he saw her, the liquor shop incident, the slap, everything.

'I love her, Nana. But I am too scared to tell her and ruin everything we have. I don't know how she feels about me.'

His nana smiled at him.

'I know exactly how you feel. I've gone through the same emotions when I was your age. And let me tell you from experience, it's always better to talk to the other person than keep your feelings bottled up inside you.'

'But what if that person doesn't feel the same way about you?' asked Sidharth.

'Then you can continue to live as friends. I know it will be a challenge, but isn't it better than living a lie? Telling her that you love her can also open the doors to a new life full of infinite possibilities. There are only two primary emotions that govern human beings—love and fear. You can either live in love or live in fear. And you, cannot feel these two emotions together, at exactly the same time. If we're in fear, we are not in a place of love. When we're in a place of love, we cannot be in a place of fear. You have to decide what you want.'

Nana left the room, giving him much to think about.

I don't want to live in a place of fear. I want to feel love; I want to feel her by my side. I want to feel everything that one feels in love. I love you. I love you, Avni,' he screamed in his head.

He was now determined to propose to Avni, whatever be the outcome. He called up Sonal and Bani to tell them about his plan. He was going to propose to her straight after the exam the next day. Both of them were delighted at the idea and promised to be there in support.

~

The next morning, he left his house wearing a blue T-shirt. He knew it was her favourite colour. The exam was at 10:30 a.m., and Sidharth had messaged Avni that they should start from home earlier than usual.

Avni had gone to Nani's place before the exam to take her blessings.

'Nani, today is the last exam, so wish me luck,' she said sitting beside her grandmother as she rested on the bed.

'Beta, my best wishes are always with you. And I know you will do well, with or without my blessings.'

'No . . . your blessings are my lucky charm.'

'Then I'll shower more blessings on you if you bring phirni on your way back. I've been craving to eat it since yesterday. Maybe because next week is your nana's death anniversary and phirni was his favourite sweet.'

'Nani, sweets are not good for you.'

'Please, can't you do this much for me? And a little bit of phirni won't harm me.'

'You're diabetic, and your sugar is already on the higher side. Mom told me that it recently shot up, didn't it?'

'Oh, your mother talks rubbish. Come on, just once. I am missing your nana and want to have his favourite dish. It will not kill me; it will make me feel better. Trust me,' she said, recalling old memories. 'You know, when he had come to see me for the first time, I had made phirni, not knowing that it was his favourite sweet dish. One taste of my phirni and he said yes to our match.'

'How come you never told me this before?' Avni asked in surprise. 'So he said yes to you only because you made him some amazing phirni?'

'Yes, I'll tell you the longer version of this story after your exam. But only after you bring some phirni for me,' she said with a child-like pleasure.

'Hey Bhagwaan, you and your phirni. Ok, I'll bring it. But not a word to Mom. And nothing sweet after this, promise?'

'Yes, promise. Now go, or you'll be late. All the best for your exam.'

Avni took her blessings and rushed out. When she reached the college, Sidharth's heart skipped a beat on seeing her. He had never felt like this before.

'Avni, I want to talk to you after the exam. So don't rush back home immediately, OK?'

'What about?' she asked, as she read through her notes one final time.

'Not now. After the exam. It's something I've wanted to say for a very long time.'

Avni looked up from her notes and gave him a warm smile. That was all the hope and confidence he needed. They headed to the exam hall and wished each other luck before taking their respective seats. Sidharth submitted his answer paper a few minutes before time and waited for Avni and the others outside the classroom. Once everyone was out, Avni asked him, 'How did your paper go?'

'It was okay,' Sidharth replied.

Bani's eyes were locked on the question paper. 'Almost, 70 per cent of the question paper was set from those three fucking chapters that I didn't bother studying. It's a fucking conspiracy against me. The same thing happened in the last paper.'

Sidharth couldn't be bothered about the question paper. He turned to Avni and said, 'I have something to talk to you about.'

'Oh yes, what about?'

'Not here. Let's go to the parking area,' Sidharth suggested. Avni walked to the car park with him. Just as he was about to say something, Avni received a text on her phone. She opened it and was stunned by what she read. She was shaking and almost about to collapse on the spot.

'What happened?' Sidharth asked.

'Nothing. I'll ... talk to you ... later,' Avni stammered and rushed home on her scooty.

She parked her scooty outside Nani's home and ran inside. It was a text from her dad. Nani had passed away that morning.

She rushed to her mom who was crying uncontrollably. 'After you left for the exam, she started feeling uneasy. She called us up but before we could reach, it was all over, Avni. We couldn't even take her to the hospital. Your nani is no more.'

Avni couldn't believe it. She went and sat by her nani's lifeless body, holding her cold blue hand. She was totally shattered, like someone had ripped her heart out. Her nani was her lifeline; her mentor; her friend, her everything.

This can't be true. What about the phirni I was going to get for you? What about the story of how you and Nana met? How could you just break all your promises and leave me? You're my lucky charm and I need you . . . how am I supposed to live without you?

She wanted to cry but couldn't; her parents were in tears, but she felt like her support system had been taken away from her in a blink of an eye. She was numb.

Chapter 7

I *feel emotionless, blank, hopeless, directionless. Nani's death has pulled the rug from under my feet. How am I supposed to survive without her? How can there be a world without my nani in it? It has robbed me of my ability to feel joy. Living without Nani wasn't something I'd ever considered. But it happened, the worst possible outcome—I woke up one morning in a world without Nani.*

Every night as I try to sleep, I find myself staring at the ceiling and images of her flash through my mind. I remember the things she told me, the things I shared with her. Everything. They disintegrate under my scrutiny, slipping away like sand through my desperate fingers, showing me the truth whether I want to acknowledge it or not. If only she had come to stay with us. If only I hadn't left for college that day. All my life I will be haunted by these thoughts.

I want to shout my guts out but cannot. So, I get back to bed and just weep a little. What starts with a tear turns into an uncontrollable flow of emotions. She appears before me when I open my phone's gallery, smiling and healthy. Nani is real on the screen, but when I put my phone down, I am acutely aware that she is fading from the world's memory, though never from mine. I keep staring at the night sky hoping for a sign that she exists beyond the realm of the physical world. And I hope and pray that she is in a better place, wherever she is.

Nani's death left Avni devastated. She had disconnected herself from everything, crying for hours alone in her room, staring at their pictures together, and breaking into uncontrollable sobs every time the realization hit her that Nani was no longer around. She was barely eating and had stopped interacting with people. This continued for the couple of months, and she woke up daily with the thought that she wouldn't be able to face the world. She missed college often and avoided meeting her friends. Her parents thought it best to leave her be for some time. They knew she needed time to heal. The grief continued to consume her little by little. She had to use every ounce of strength she possessed to get to college on the day the exam results were announced.

It was around 7 p.m., and there was a huge rush to see the results displayed on the notice board. Sidharth and Avni were standing at a safe distance from the crowd, while Sonal and Bani tried to jostle for space in front of the notice board. They came back after a while with their exam results.

'So what is it?' Sidharth asked Bani in a tense voice.

'I have two KTs,' Bani revealed in a subdued voice that she had failed in two subjects.

'I have passed all the exams. Sidharth, you have topped, as was expected of you,' added Sonal.

Sidharth didn't care for his own results. 'And what about Avni?'

Both Sonal and Bani looked at Avni and said, 'Three KTs. The last three . . .'

Avni was aghast and walked off without a word. Sidharth and Sonal ran after her, but she insisted she wanted to be left alone for some time. She wasn't able to give her best in the last three exams, but she had thought she would at least clear them, if nothing else. It was the first time she had failed at anything and didn't know how to deal with it. First Nani's passing and now this. Could life get any worse?

When Sidharth reached home and disclosed the results to his mother and grandfather, they were elated. His nana enveloped him in a tight embrace but Sidharth pushed him away. He was in no mood for celebrations.

He went straight to his balcony to check on Avni but the lights in her room were switched off. Worried, Sidharth sent her a text.

Are you okay? Please don't think about the exam results. You can easily cover up in the next semester. And please take care of yourself. I know you're going through hell right now, but nothing is more important than your health.

The message got delivered but she didn't read it. He tried calling her but her phone was switched off. She hadn't gone home after college. She just wandered on the streets, feeling utterly directionless, like a boat caught in a storm. The semester results had pulled her rapidly to the bottom of the sea. She was so lost that she had unknowingly walked to Nani's apartment. It was only when she saw the house locked that she comprehended that Nani was no more. She felt herself overcome with grief as tears rolled down her eyes.

She sat by the entrance to the house and said, *I miss you Nani, I wish you were here with me. I always knew that losing you would be difficult but I didn't realize it would be this difficult. I feel like dying. I want to end this agony. You had told me not to get too attached to anyone, but what about my attachment for you? Ever since your passing, I have been waking up in the middle of the night with panic attacks. How am I supposed to live without you, Nani? This wound you have left me with might never heal.*

She reached home many hours later. Her parents were worried sick about her and asked her where she'd been. She ran to her mom and hugged her. In between sobs, she told her about her exam results. Her mom calmed her down and made her sit beside her. Her dad placed a comforting hand on her head and said, 'Its fine, beta. You can't always be perfect at everything, right? Failures are as important as successes.'

Her mom ran her fingers through Avni's hair.

'You'll be fine. Don't overburden yourself unnecessarily. We know how difficult Nani's death has been for you. Be around your friends, talk to us if you feel like it, but don't lock yourself in your room and behave like a zombie. It's been difficult for all of us but we need to recover from it. Time heals all wounds.'

Her mom smiled and pulled her closer for a hug. Avni hugged her back, but she still missed the warm, comforting hugs of her nani. She wiped her tears away and went to her room.

The next day, Sonal reached Avni's house to convince her to come to college, although Avni didn't want to. Her parents insisted she go—college would be a welcome distraction and would make her feel better. Avni took a quick bath, changed her clothes and left for college. Before the first lecture could commence, her class-in-charge called her to his cabin saying he wanted to have a word with her in private.

'You must have seen your results by now,' he said.

Avni was too embarrassed to say anything and kept looking at the floor. The professor continued.

'You are a brilliant student and are also a part of the student committee. Focus more on your studies and less on frivolous stuff. These are the most important years of your life.'

'I know, Sir. I haven't been keeping well,' she replied.

'I understand. I basically called you here to tell that your attendance is quite low this semester. You need to start attending college more regularly if you are to be allowed to sit for the next set of exams. You're a good student and I would hate to see you lose out.'

'Yes, Sir,' Avni responded.

Avni wanted someone to talk to, someone who would really listen without judgement, without giving her unwanted advice. Everyone around her kept telling that she would be fine but that was the last thing she wanted to hear. To make matters worse, her college mates left no opportunity to make her feel like a failure.

'Didn't she have like 80 per cent attendance in the last semester? That just goes on to prove that attending lectures is worthless.'

'She used to spend the whole day inside the library. I'm so glad I didn't waste my time there.'

People might forget your birthday, but they won't forget how badly you fare in exams. Avni tried her best to ignore them but the taunts continued.

She wanted to scream and say 'I'm not okay'. She didn't want solutions to her problems. She didn't want people to try to make her happy. She just wanted to *feel* okay. But she wasn't sure what being okay was any more. She wished she could just disappear into the darkness that surrounded her.

One day she was sitting in the college lawns with Sidharth. They were bunking the maths lecture. Sonal and Bani had low attendance in the subject and had told Sidharth and Avni they would join them once it was over. Sidharth could see the sadness in Avni's eyes. He moved a little closer to her and said,

'Can I ask you something?'

Avni turned towards him without saying anything. Her pale face was heartbreaking for Sidharth to see. The sparkle in her eyes had been replaced by dark circles.

'If your grandmother was here, what would you talk to her about?'

'She'll never be back,' Avni said in a heavy voice.

'I know. And you need to move on. How do you think it makes her feel to see you like this? I know it's quite easy for me to say this, but just think about the good times with her, think about all the life advice she gave you, think that she didn't have to undergo any complications in the last phase of her life. She was a good soul and her soul departed peacefully. Now by being sad and hopeless, aren't you troubling her soul? Wouldn't you want her to rest in peace?'

Avni thought for a moment and said, 'You know, if Nani was here, she would tell me to ignore the ones who don't matter and only listen to the ones that do.' She broke into a smile thinking of her nani.

She had barely spoken in the last few months and to see her smile was such a relief to Sidharth.

'Now that's more like it. Let me take a mental picture of this moment before you go back to being glum,' he teased. 'You know my relatives in Gujarat have always waited for my results. Not because they care for me but because they want something to talk about. Once, when I was in the eleventh standard, I got terrible scores. And suddenly everyone pretended they were worried for me. They would call up my mom and say stuff like, "he is losing his focus, junior college has gone to his head; he should concentrate more on his studies, the boards are just around the corner", and so on. Even relatives I have never met would call up my mom and say all kinds of rubbish, like I'd taken an education loan from them or something.'

Avni broke into a laugh. He wanted to take a picture of her in that moment and show her how beautiful she looked. Just then, DK and the gang came to congratulate him for topping the class, pressing him to throw a party.

'Just a thank you is not going to work. We need to celebrate big. Call us when you are free.' The gang waved at him and left. Avni wasn't happy seeing them, and the mention of the exam results made her retreat into her shell once again.

After college, Sidharth met with DK and The Big Bikers to celebrate. But the main reason for his meeting wasn't celebration. He wanted to ask DK if there was some way one could clear the papers using a source at the university. But DK laughed at the suggestion.

'If there was a source, you think I would have repeated the year?'

'You know that Avni failed in the last three exams. It breaks my heart to see her suffer like this. I love her and just want to see her happy.'

'But does she love you?' DK asked.

'I don't care if she does. I love her and that's all that matters,' Sidharth replied.

If Avni had sleepless nights over her nani's untimely demise, so did Sidharth. He couldn't see her suffer such agony, and knew he had to get her out of her misery at any cost.

With time, Avni's depression got worse. Her friends and family were her lifeline, and were doing everything in their power to help her. Her parents even consulted a doctor who gave her anti-depressants after a diagnosis and asked her to come for regular therapy sessions. But it was a constant battle between her will and her anxieties. Sadly, her anxieties always overpowered everything else.

She put on a smiling face for everyone to see, while the storm continued to rage inside her, destroying her bit by bit. She tried to put on a brave front for her parents, but some days she didn't even have the energy to fake a smile. She didn't want people to see her as a miserable person. She knew she was strong, but why did she always feel so damn weak? Nothing about her life seemed to be going right. Her inner demons took her down further and further into the abyss.

It was another one of those nights when she woke up with a fright. She had had a nightmare and was shivering and crying. Her mom, who had begun to sleep with her, quickly fetched her a glass of water. Her dad came into the room, hearing her loud wails.

'Why are you taking so much stress? Do you want to take a break from college?'

'I don't know, Dad.'

Her dad held her hand and said, 'You always asked us why we live a carefree life, right?' For precisely this reason. See what exam pressure has done to you. You can't let it snatch your happiness like this. There are more things to life than just this. Look how we've found a way to find relief from our worries. Be it our obsession for games or making videos, they act as stress busters.'

Her mom added, 'He is right. Being carefree isn't a bad thing if you aren't careless. We realized it way too early, and gradually cultivated an attitude that didn't take the fun away from our lives. There will be phases where you feel low and that's absolutely fine, but as long as you keep yourself involved in something that keeps you busy, something that makes you feel happy and alive, things will eventually be fine.'

'Do you want to go on a vacation?' her dad suggested.

'No Dad, I am okay. I will take some time, that's all. I have accepted that Nani is gone forever. I have told myself I will do better in the exams the next time, but this feeling of constant sadness just doesn't leave me. I try hard to keep myself motivated, and I wish I could get over things as easily as you guys, but it's not so easy. Anyway, all I can say is that I'm trying.'

The next day she went to college in a slightly better mood. It was a lecture on communication skills, and each student was made to give a presentation elaborating on the '7Cs in business correspondence'. Bani was late and the professor saw her entering the lecture hall from the back door.

'Miss Bani, why don't you come to the front of the class and start the presentation? You can ask your friends what the topic of the presentation is.'

Bani asked Sidharth, who decided to play a prank on her. 'You have to speak about why you chose engineering.'

Sidharth and Sonal giggled as Bani walked to where the professor was standing. Even Avni had a smile on her face.

'Engineering happened by chance; everyone around me was taking engineering and so I opted for it as well. But now I realize how much value it adds to my life, even in everyday affairs. When a fan doesn't work at home, everyone at home looks at me to repair it. When my dad's bike doesn't start, he asks me to fix it instead of taking it to the workshop. When the water gets blocked in a tap, my mother knows I can sort it out in seconds. I have become everyone's go-to mechanic at home.'

The whole class broke into fits of laughter. It was only when the professor intervened that she realized she had messed up big time. She went back to her seat extremely embarrassed.

'How was it?' Sidharth teased.

'Oh fuck off. You'll be the last person I will ever ask for anything.' Bani wanted to bang his head against the wall.

Avni was next. Sidharth was keen to hear her as she was a good orator. But when she stood in front of the entire class, she completely lost her train of thought. Her confidence seemed to have flown out of the window and without speaking a word, she returned back to her seat. Sidharth was stunned to see what had become of the girl who had once impressed everyone in the college committee with her oratory skills. He felt miserable seeing her like this. He knew he had to do something before it was too late.

That's it. I cannot take it any more, she thought to herself in the local train on the western line while going to the coaching centre after college that day. Standing by the door, she ignored Sonal's pleas to come back to her seat. She kept staring at the passing tracks thinking:

I've tried many times to fight this, even going so far as asking help from friends, family and doctors. Nonetheless, nothing has worked. I feel certain that I am going mad. I am trying hard to hide but there is nowhere I can hide. There's no escape. It feels like I can never get away from this fate; there's nothing I can do to change it. I am also trying hard to hide my struggles but I am afraid that the people who are close to me know too much and I don't want to bring them down with me. I am afraid I'll hurt them and subconsciously I am pushing them away. I know it's wrong and its crushing my being but I have lost control. No one can understand what I am going through. I feel isolated, alone and unloved. I feel I can't handle this terrible time. Will the world accept the broken version of me or is it better to burn out than fade away? Because some days I just wish that I didn't have to talk to anyone. That I could just be left alone. Left for dead.

Avni felt like she was being forged in a fire. It seemed that she'd have to melt completely before she could become strong again!

Chapter 8

*N*o storm lasts forever. You just need someone to guide
you through it and help anchor you to life! I'll be that
someone in Avni's life.

Sidharth typed these lines on his phone's notepad,
took a screenshot and put it up as his phone's wallpaper.
He wanted to be reminded of this continually. He had
already made a to-do list and was confident he could
get her out of her depressed state. The first thing on the
list was her birthday, and he wanted to make her feel
really special on that day. He was discussing his plans
with Bani and Sonal in college the next day when Sonal
revealed something about Avni's past.

'She has gone through this phase once before as well,
when Prince had passed away all of a sudden. I think we
were in the eighth standard at that time.'

'Prince?' Sidharth asked with a raised eyebrow.

'Ya, her pet Labrador. He was more than family to them. She was traumatized by his death. She cannot cope with deaths of loved ones. First Prince and now her nani. Her nani was her lifeline.'

'I have an idea but I am not sure if it will work. There's no harm in trying it though,' said Sidharth, and shared his idea with the girls.

The idea was exciting and the girls promised to lend their support in helping Sidharth execute it to perfection. And isn't friendship all about supporting each other in good times and bad?

~

Sidharth checked the time on his watch. It was 11:45 p.m. He was wearing Avni's favourite blue T-shirt. He took the customized cake he had ordered especially for Avni and sneaked out of his house. His mother was sleeping and he didn't want her to know that he was going to Avni's house in the dead of the night. She still hadn't warmed to her and did not like his son spending too much time with her when he could be using that time to study. Sonal was already waiting outside and Bani was on her way with the special gift that Sidharth had asked her to get. He had informed Avni's dad in advance that they would be coming and, just five minutes before twelve, he messaged him.

Uncle, we are outside, please open the door.

Balwinder asked Mona to see to it that Avni didn't come near the main door. He opened the door and welcomed both of them inside.

'Let's make the arrangements quickly,' he instructed.

Sidharth nodded and placed the cake on the centre table. Bani was yet to reach and that worried Sidharth. He wanted to present the gift to Avni as soon as she stepped out of her room. He texted Bani again.

At least today you could have been on time. He sent the message to her along with an angry emoji. As the clock struck twelve, Avni's mom called her outside. Avni was shocked to see Sidharth and Sonal cheering for her and singing happy birthday in unison. She was led to the cake, which had a miniature doll on it that resembled her. Her hands were open in a wide embrace, as if waiting to hug someone. The cake and the doll brought an unexpected smile to her face.

She cut the cake and fed the first piece to her parents, followed by Sidharth.

'This is beautiful,' she said pointing towards the doll. She knew only he could pull off something like this.

Sidharth wished her and gave her a special note that he had written for her.

Do you know why little Avni is standing with her arms wide open? Because she is ready to embrace life once again. Avni, I want you to know that no matter where you are in life, no matter how bleak your situation, this is not the end of your story. You have to promise us that by your next birthday, you will be gleaming and full of life, just like your miniature doll.

Avni looked at him with tears in her eyes and whispered a thank you. She knew the lengths he had gone to make her feel special on her birthday.

Just then, there was a knock on the door.

'Close your eyes. There's another surprise for you,' Sidharth told her. Bani was finally here with the special gift.

'Why?' Avni asked curiously.

'Just do as I say.'

'I am sorry for being late,' apologized Bani, trying to catch her breath.

'It's okay,' Sidharth replied and took the gift from her.

'Now open your eyes, Avni.'

Avni opened her eyes and shrieked in happiness. Sidharth was standing in front of her holding a black Labrador pup in a small basket. When Sonal had told him about Prince, Sidharth had the perfect idea for a birthday gift. They had gone to the nearest animal shelter and adopted a cute little black Lab for Avni.

'This little cutie pie is all yours,' Sidharth said, and handed the basket over to Avni.

Avni was beaming with joy and Sidharth couldn't have been happier than he was in that moment.

She named him 'Junior' and played with him all night, even after everyone had left. She texted Sidharth before sleeping.

I don't know how to thank you. You've made my day so special. Thank you!

Sidharth texted her back.

Anything for you. You're a rock star.

Sidharth wanted to give Avni all the happiness in the world. Avni smiled when she read Sidharth's message.

The next morning, she opened the curtains of her room and saw Sidharth standing in the balcony. She held the pup in her hands and made him wave at Sidharth, making him smile. Sidharth had planned more surprises for her that he would reveal through the course of the day. He signalled to her to pick up the phone.

'Hi,' Avni greeted him.

'Get ready, we are going to Marine Drive. Sonal and Bani are coming too,' Sidharth said.

'What? Why?'

'I am not asking you; I am telling you. Get ready. I'll pick you up in half an hour.' Sidharth hung up.

Avni was slightly hesitant to go, but her friends had done so much for her that she didn't have the heart to say no. Sidharth had booked an Uber. His mother wasn't pleased and tried to oppose him, but he had made up his mind and once the Uber arrived, he tiptoed out of the house.

They took the cab and left for Sonal's house. In the car, Sidharth took out a surprise from his bag. It was a dreamcatcher.

'Another small gift for you. Happy birthday once again.'

'Just like this dreamcatcher, I want you to continue to chase your dreams. Like your nani, even this will give you hope and strength. So start dreaming big, and don't limit yourself to dreaming about the things you are good at. You never know what future holds for you.'

Avni gazed at him with a look of genuine affection. She could see that he cared for her unconditionally. But was there something more to it? She recollected how Sidharth had been with her like a true friend. Whatever it was, she felt much better that day than she had in the last few months.

'What happened?' Sidharth asked seeing Avni lost in thought.

'Why are you doing all this?' she asked turning to look at him.

'I just want to see that sparkling smile back on your face. You know you look very beautiful when you smile, don't you?'

Avni didn't say anything. She looked outside the window but couldn't stop thinking about what he said. They picked up Sonal and Bani and, within a couple of hours, found themselves on Marine Drive. They had sandwiches and juice at Bachelors and sat by the sea, feeling the gentle sea breeze on their faces.

'You guys should have gone to college today. Wasting time and doing nothing isn't right,' Avni said.

'Oh, look who's talking. The girl who has hardly attended any lectures this semester,' Sonal remarked.

'My case is different,' Avni replied.

Sidharth intervened saying, 'Sometimes, it's OK to do nothing. You shouldn't be made to feel guilty about gazing at the sea, binge-watching a web series, hanging out with friends or playing games. Sometimes defocusing gives you a better perspective on life.'

Avni turned to look at him.

His thoughts made her think about her own beliefs. They spent the rest of the day gossiping about the professors, roaming around the city and doing silly things. The studious girl that she was, it wasn't often that she had hung out with her friends, and Avni was loving every moment of it. After everything Sidharth had done for her, she had finally warmed up to him and was grateful for his friendship and company.

She came back home and hung the dreamcatcher near her window. After playing with Junior for some time, she picked up the phone to send a 'thank you' message to Sidharth. But before she could type, she received a message from him.

I hope you had fun today. I am so grateful for your friendship and I just want you to know that I am so proud of you for trying to break out of your shell. No one's perfect. Everyone has their own little flaws. Even I do. I am a flawed son. A flawed neighbour. A flawed friend. We are a sum of both our strengths and weaknesses. Continue to smile because your smile adds so much charm to my day!

Avni started to blush. She knew where the conversation was headed. She sent him a thank you text and shut her eyes. It was the first time in months that she slept peacefully at night, with Junior next to her.

~

Since her birthday, Sidharth and Avni had started spending more and more time together, be it in the college campus or at her house. Like the minute hand of the clock moves gradually, she was moving on, but she wasn't able to completely get over the depression, which haunted her every now and then. Sidharth knew she was still affected, and wanted her to feel absolutely fine. Thus one day Sidharth decided to take her for a surprise visit to a place that was close to his grandfather's heart.

The previous night, he had discussed the entire plan with Nana.

'Nana, I am sure that her wounds will heal once we take her there. You have been there a couple of times since we have shifted here and I know how much you love that place.'

'That's a great idea. Let's go there tomorrow. I'll talk to Mr Wagle, who is the owner of that place. We were colleagues when I was posted in Vapi. Now, after retirement, he dedicates all his time to it.'

'Thank you, Nana. You are awesome.' Sidharth hugged him and immediately texted Avni.

We're bunking the morning classes tomorrow. We'll only attend the afternoon practicals. And don't say no, for you're coming along with me.

Avni replied: *Where? And what happened all of a sudden?*

I am not telling you anything now. See you in the morning, Sidharth texted back.

Around 10 a.m., as soon as Sidharth's mother left for the temple, Sidharth booked a cab and asked Avni to come down. When she came out, she saw Sidharth standing near the door with his grandfather. She hadn't expected to see him there.

'How are you, Beta? Are you feeling better now?' his nana asked.

'I am much better, Nana. Thank you.' She smiled, and looking at Sidharth asked, 'What's the plan?'

Sidharth didn't want to say anything just yet. He asked her to trust him, and they all got into the cab. Soon they reached their destination. Avni got out and read the board outside the entrance to the building. It said 'The Happy Club'.

'I have never been to this place. Where are we?' she asked.

'It's a home for retired officers who don't have a family or whose children have abandoned them. It's run by a friend of my nana's, and today they are celebrating the tenth anniversary of the Happy Club . . .

They stepped inside and saw that the entire place was decorated with balloons. There was an open garden in front of the building where Wagle was waiting to welcome them.

'Hello, Jailor Sahib. How are you?' asked Mr Wagle.

'Wagle, why do you insist on calling me that?' Sidharth's nana asked, amused.

'Jailor Sahib carries weight, my dear friend,' he replied and looked towards Sidharth and Avni, 'How are you young chaps?'

'This is my grandson Sidharth, and this is Avni, his friend,' Nana said, introducing them.

'Friend or girlfriend?' Wagle teased.

Sidharth and Avni didn't know which way to look.

'Come in please, I'll introduce you to the others,' Mr Wagle said and ushered them inside, 'We are fifteen retired officers who are living our second innings here. We're all like family now. We live together, laugh together, cry on each other's shoulders and most importantly, enjoy whatever time remains.'

Just then, a man in his late fifties walked towards Avni and exclaimed, 'You are beautiful!'

Avni was taken aback and, as he came up to her, she had goosebumps. She observed that everyone was staring at her like she had committed a crime.

As soon as he said that, all the others in the room started clapping and hooting for him. Avni couldn't understand what was going on.

'I'm so sorry. These guys had dared me to say this to you. Though I did mean what I said. You are pretty.'

Sidharth started laughing and Avni couldn't help but smile too.

'I am Daniel D'Souza,' he said introducing himself.

'Avni,' she replied. Soon, others walked up to them and everyone started chatting. They cut the cake a little later, and started dancing to Bollywood music. Avni was amazed to see how full of life they were, even after such hardships. Mr Wagle pulled Sidharth and Avni onto the dance floor. Avni was reluctant at first.

Wagle turned to Sidharth and said, 'She's your friend, you should tell her to dance with you. Come on, it's a celebration, not a funeral.'

The echo of her slap was still fresh in Sidharth's mind. Avni could sense his discomfort at being on the dance floor with her. She pinched him, making his heart beat faster. It was the first time she had touched him. After much coaxing by everyone, they joined the others on the dance floor.

Once the celebrations were over, Avni took a seat next to Sidharth's nana and Mr Wagle. Sidharth was busy chatting with Daniel and the other retired officers. When Avni told Sidharth's nana why she had been feeling depressed for the last few months, he narrated an incident to her.

'I still remember a friend of mine called Rakesh. He always got whatever he desired for. He worked in a big company with a handsome package, and led a fairly luxurious life. I, on the other hand, was struggling at my job, barely able to support my family. Every time I would meet him, I would look at him with jealousy. He went to parties, flirted around with girls and led a carefree life. The only people I could flirt around with were the criminals in jail. But I continued to stay mentally strong. Eventually, Rakesh got divorced, all his investment in shares failed and he got addicted to drugs. There came a point when he lost everything he had worked for and that's when I realized that everyone has their own struggles. You just have to face whatever life throws at you.'

Avni understood what he was trying to say. It was like her nani was explaining things to her all over again.

She felt an instant connection with him. He exuded the same warmth as Nani.

'Nanaji, I'd like to continue talking to you after today, if that's okay with you?' she asked.

Nana held her hand and said, 'You called me Nana, right? Then you don't need permission to meet me. You can share whatever is in your heart, whenever you want.'

Avni took a deep breath and said, 'I don't know. I always feel that I would lose out on something if I don't stay competitive or make plans for tomorrow. And when I hit rock bottom, I felt that I had lost track of life, and would never keep pace with others.'

Mr Wagle, who was patiently listening all the while, jumped in, 'That's the problem with your generation. You have forgotten to live.' He paused and then said, 'I was no different from you, and that's the reason I understand how wrong that approach is. When I was young, I could never live in the moment. I always thought that I should strive for a better tomorrow. When I was in school, I dreamed of getting into a good college. When I got into one, I dreamed of getting placed in a good company. Then marriage, kids and their education. It was only one day when my wife passed away, I thought about my life's journey and realized that I had never taken the time to savour the special moments that filled my days.

I never enjoyed the successes; I never appreciated the things my wife did for me; nor did I create moments with her that I could relive now. In the quest of a better tomorrow, I lost touch with the present. My whole life passed before my eyes without giving me the chance to enjoy it. I began to feel empty inside. I have missed the gift of living, and that's when I started my second innings, my Happy Club.'

Mr Wagle concluded by saying, 'Don't let this boy go. He loves you a lot. I've seen it in his eyes. You're very lucky to have him in your life. Jailor Sahib told me how he was constantly by your side when you were depressed. It's very rare to find a person like that. If you have even the slightest feelings for him, don't overlook them.'

Avni looked in Sidharth's direction. He was busy laughing and having a good time with the officers. He looked at her staring at him and asked if something was wrong. She smiled and said nothing. Her smile expressed her inner feelings. Sidharth continued to entertain everyone present. Looking at him, a strange sensation erupted inside her. Was she starting to have feelings for Sidharth? The thought scared her but also made her feel good. Her perception towards love and life had changed. There was no escaping the pull she was feeling towards him with each passing day. It was his love that gave her the power to overcome the fear that had been tormenting her for months. Like fire, he burnt her fears down and ignited happiness and courage in her. Even she wasn't aware that it would crush her beliefs and light the spark of love.

Chapter 9

Sidharth and Avni left for college directly from the Happy Club. Mr Wagle's words resonated in her mind as she sat next to Sidharth in the auto.

'I hope you liked the visit to the Happy Club. You look much happier now,' observed Sidharth.

'I wish I could have met these people before. I realized that my problems and worries are nothing compared to theirs. They've gone through so much, and still lead their lives with a smile on their faces. I was shattered after Nani's death. There were times when I didn't want to get out of bed. I thank my parents, who stood by me and never put any additional pressure on me. And you as well. Were it not for your constant prodding and encouragement, I would not have stepped out of my room. So thank you for supporting me and always being there for me.'

'Damn, that was one hell of an award-winning speech!'

Avni laughed at his remark and looked at him.

'Can I ask you something?'

'Of course,' Sidharth replied awkwardly.

'Why did you do all this? And I want an honest answer.'

'Because ever since I've met you, my world has turned upside down. I get excited at the mere thought of spending more time with you. I can't think of anything but you. I love you, Avni.'

'I think I have fallen in love with you too,' she replied, slightly embarrassed as she acknowledged it.

Sidharth was speechless. He realized he was only daydreaming when Avni snapped her fingers at him.

'Hello, where are you lost? Will you answer my question?'

Fuck, I thought it was happening for real.

'I did nothing. I just didn't want to see you looking so sad and upset all the time. You know you look your best when you smile, don't you?'

Avni wasn't satisfied with his answer and repeated her question, 'So, you won't tell me, right?'

'Tell you what?' Sidharth pretended as if he didn't understand what she meant.

'The truth,' Avni said loud and clear.

'I just did.'

'Okay then, I'll wait for you to tell me some other day.' She was leaving him all these opportunities to reveal his true feelings for her but he just didn't seem to be taking the hint.

It's amazing how she had fallen in love with a person she didn't even notice the first time she met. In fact, she detested him for the first couple of meetings. But now he had become such an integral part of her world that she couldn't imagine spending a single day without him. What was happening to her? Was it really love?

~

The whole evening Sidharth couldn't think of anything but Avni's question.

What did she want me to say? Did she want me to tell her that I love her? Was she hinting that she loved me back?

Sidharth took a deep breath and left her a WhatsApp message.

'Hi, can we talk?'

Avni was feeding Junior when she saw the message. Holding the pup in one hand, she sent him a voice note. 'I'm with Junior. Do you want to meet him?'

She sent him a picture of Junior chomping on his food, with the caption, 'My dinner companion. Did you have your dinner?'

Sidharth replied, 'He he, cute. I just got done with dinner. Can we talk now?'

'About what?' Avni knew what he was referring to but wanted to keep playing the guessing game.

'You wanted to know why I was doing all this for you. I think I'm ready to tell you why.'

Sidharth could see her typing a reply.

'I am sure you're going to say the same thing you said in the afternoon,' Avni texted back.

'No. I will tell you the truth.'

'Okay, go on.'

Sidharth took a long time to type how he was feeling.

'I'm not sure if I can put into words how I feel, but I have to say something. If I don't say it now, I will never be able to say it. I have never felt as good as I feel around you. If you are sad, my days are dull; if you are happy, my days are bright. I have felt an instant connection with you since the day I saw you outside your house in the car. And when I got to know you a little better, I was even more attracted to you. You're simple, honest and caring, and so different from all the other girls in the city. All I want to do is be around you and make you happy.'

He reread the message umpteen times before sending it. Then he immediately regretted having sent the message, and threw his phone on the bed. The minute it buzzed, he grabbed it.

'So, what does all this mean?' Avni had messaged back.

He felt relieved that she wasn't furious with him. He was about to reply when Sonal called him.

'Dude, what the fuck is wrong with you?' she said.

'What happened? Is everything all right?'

'Idiot, I am asking about Avni. You are messaging her right?' Sonal said.

How the fuck does she know? Avni told Sonal already?

'She forwarded your message to me. What the hell have you done?'

'What happened?' Sidharth asked sounding worried. 'Did I do something wrong?'

'You are so dumb. How were you able to change her perception towards love? She has only spoken about you for the last couple of hours. She knows that you are going to propose to her and that's the fucking reason I called you. If you don't tell her now, you won't be able to tell her ever.'

Sidharth was thrilled to hear this. 'What else did she say to you?'

'I am not going to spoil the fun. Just go ahead and do it today.' And with that, Sonal hung up.

Sonal's words boosted his confidence. He texted Avni and asked her to come to her window. He took out his white slate board from his drawer, then got the battery-operated string and red fairy lights from near his desk and created a border around the slate. With a marker, he wrote the message he wanted to convey.

Then, he switched off the room lights to put the entire focus on the slate.

He checked his mobile. There was one unread message from Avni. 'I am already at the window. Your room is dark. I cannot see you.'

He asked her to shut her eyes, and switched on the string lights.

When Avni opened her eyes, she saw Sidharth standing with a slate in his hand. She read the message.

'Avni, I love you. Will you be mine forever?'

She nodded and called him up immediately. 'Do you mean it?' she asked.

'I do! I love you so much, Avni.'

She looked at the life mantra framed on the wall. *Never get too attached to someone.* It was too late for that.

Avni sat down on the bed and whispered to him over the phone, 'I can't believe this is really happening. Am I dreaming?'

'This is reality, Avni. I want to hold your hand and be with you for eternity. When I am with you, time flies, but when we are apart, I crave to see you every second. I never thought in my wildest dreams that you would ever say yes to me. I am so blessed to have you in my life. All I want you to do is come here and kiss me on the same cheek on which you slapped me,' he teased.

'Shut up and sleep. Good night.'

'Just good night?'

'Okay, I love you. Happy?'

'Not really. I want a kiss too.'

'No, not now.'

'Please,' Sidharth pleaded.

'Now bye. That's enough for tonight.'

~

The next morning, the first thing Sidharth did after getting up was to text Avni and ask her to come to her window. Then he went out to his balcony and called her.

'I want you to be the first thing I see every morning, my beautiful Chotu.'

'Chotu?' Avni asked surprised.

'I'm going to call you Chotu from today because you are just like a cute, innocent little kid.'

Avni smiled, 'Call me whatever you want. Now get ready, and I'll see you soon.'

'Wear your red dress today. I love that dress and that colour on you.' He still remembered how ravishing she had looked in the dress during the fresher's party.

'Oh, so you notice the dresses I wear?' Avni asked.

'I notice everything about you. You are all over my phone gallery.'

'I am all over your life now.'

When Avni finally stepped out in the red dress, Sidharth couldn't help but smile. He wanted to run to her and give her a tight hug. He wanted to play with her hair and kiss her soft cheeks.

Once they were at a safe distance from their houses, Avni parked her scooty in one of the paid parking spots Sidharth had directed her to, and came and sat behind him on his bike. Sidharth looked at her through the rear-view mirror as she tightened her grip around him. She was the first girl to ever sit on his bike, and just her mere touch sent shockwaves through him. A single touch from her and he knew what electricity was.

'I still can't accept that its true,' Sidharth said to Avni.

'I can't either. I would have been drowning in a pool of misery had you not come and rescued me in time. You mean a lot to me. I love you.'

'I love you too,' replied Sidharth.

They had reached the extreme end of the college parking lot. After alighting from the bike, Sidharth walked in with Avni by his side. Avni was holding her bag in the left hand so he caught hold of her right hand and entwined his fingers with hers. He was conscious of his hands being sweaty but Avni didn't seem to mind. He tightened his grip on her and she turned around to look at him.

They were just about to exit the parking space when they saw Sonal and Bani walking towards them. Both smiled looking at them holding hands in a public space for the first time.

'Did you tell them about us?' Sidharth asked Avni.

'I told Sonal last night and am sure she must have told Bani.'

Sonal pounced on her the minute they arrived, 'So now that you have a boyfriend to drive you to college, you'll forget me? You didn't even ask if I was coming to college today.'

Avni had forgotten all about Sonal! She tried to defend herself, 'I called you a couple of times but your number wasn't reachable.'

'So now you will make all the excuses in this world, won't you?'

Avni started to apologize but Sonal cut her short. 'Chill. I was only joking. I am so happy for the both of you.'

Bani intervened. 'By the way, you can continue to hold her hand.'

'Should we go for the lectures?' Sidharth asked, trying to change the topic as they made their way towards the lecture hall.

The same campus where he studied, enjoyed and created his own little world now seemed celestial to him. The classroom had energetic vibes and he no longer felt the lectures were boring. By the end of the day, the whole campus knew they were in love. The computer programming professor was teaching coding when Sidharth sent Avni a WhatsApp message.

'Let's leave during the break. I want to spend time with you today.'

'I can't. You know my attendance is low. I'll be screwed if I bunk any more lectures. My submissions will go for a complete toss. I only have a couple of months to cover up,' Avni texted back.

'Don't worry, Sonal will sit in for you. She's already done it for me a couple of times before. Please Chotu, even if we are in the same classroom, this distance is suffocating me.'

'Let's go after college, please? Now let's concentrate on programming.'

'This professor is an idiot. Look at him, who the fuck wears sports shoes under trousers?'

'Shut up. If you know coding, then tell me something about increment operator.'

Sidharth thought for a while and replied:

While (love on u >love on anything else)

{

Love on u++;

}

After each execution, my love will be incremented for sure!

Sidharth sent her a series of hearts. He could see her smiling while reading it.

'So, we are going, right?'

'No.'

Sidharth had to think of another trick. During the break, he somehow convinced the whole class to mass bunk and Avni was left with no other option than to bunk the class and do as he wished.

'So where are we going?' She asked as she took her place behind him on his bike.

'Juhu beach,' Sidharth answered.

'Do you even know the way to the beach? You aren't a Mumbaikar,' Avni mocked him.

'Eight months are more than enough to know every little corner of a city. And anyway, I have my GPS on.' Sidharth smiled.

They were on their way when Avni got a message from Sonal saying the mass bunk plan had failed.

The lecture is on. A couple of first benchers ditched us at the last moment. They entered the classroom as soon as the professor went in. And that bastard too started taking the lecture. In no time, the class was back on.

Avni relayed the information to Sidharth but he refused to go back.

'These dumbasses will never grow up. There's absolutely no unity in our branch,' he complained. 'A bill still has a chance to get passed in Lok Sabha but mass bunk in engineering is just a myth.'

Avni didn't feel like going back but she said nothing to Sidharth. She could feel his warmth as she tightened her grip around his waist and, with every passing minute, she felt more comfortable holding him . . . Once they reached the beach and got down from the bike, Sidharth took her hand in his and intertwined their fingers, like it was the most natural thing to do. This time there were no awkward pauses, no second thoughts, no worries about what he was doing; only him and her, and their hands fitting perfectly together. They were walking towards Juhu Chowpatty hand in hand.

'Would you like to eat something?'

'Pani puri. It's my favourite.' Her face glowed at the mere mention of pani puri.

'I know,' he said. 'Let's go to Mumbai Chaat stall. I heard their chaat is the best in town.'

'How do you know that? You are not even from around here,' Avni teased.

'DK and the biker gang told me.'

Avni didn't like Sidharth hanging out with them too much. She saw them as a nuisance and felt they would create trouble for him one day. She put these thoughts on the backburner. For now, all she wanted to do was enjoy some pani puri. She ate all six pieces in less than a minute.

'Woah. Slow down there.' He patted her head and offered her some water as she almost choked on the spicy hing water.

Sidharth picked up her complimentary masala puri and was about to gulp it down when she nudged him.

'Hey, that's mine. You ask for another one.' Avni tried to snatch it from him.

'Not until I get a kiss,' he said.

'No. You are not getting that,' Avni stated clearly.

'Then you are not getting this.' He motioned to the puri in his hand.

'Okay, eat it.' She looked away.

But Sidharth turned her towards him, and fed her the last pani puri. Avni grinned after gulping it down. He paid for it, and they walked towards the beach looking for a secluded spot where they wouldn't be disturbed. They found a quiet spot, and sat down to talk. They talked for hours about everything they possibly could. Avni also expressed her feelings and Sidharth listened to her.

'Can I ask you something?' Avni hesitantly asked.

'Yes, of course. And stop being so formal,' Sidharth replied tightening his grip on her hand.

'I don't like it when you spend the whole day with DK and his gang. Can't you let them be? I feel like they'll get you into trouble one day.'

Sidharth could feel the concern in her voice. 'They are my friends. Trust me, they are genuine. And I don't hang out with them daily. You are just getting worried unnecessarily.'

'Please, it's a request,' Avni pleaded.

'Don't worry, Chotu.' Sidharth moved closer to her. Her lips seemed warm and inviting, and it took every ounce of his strength to refrain from kissing her. Avni, on the other hand, looked like she wanted to say something, but hesitated.

'Sidharth . . .' she whispered. She was so focused on his eyes that she did not even notice how much closer he was now. Their bodies radiated so much heat that they could have set a room on fire.

He moved closer still.

It had to be her, it always was, and it always will be, he kept thinking.

'Sidharth . . .' she repeated in a soft murmur.

'I love you so much,' he whispered.

'I love you too.'

She inched closer towards him.

He cupped her face in his hands and stared into her eyes. Neither knew who made the first move, but someone did, and they were no longer two people but one. She shut her eyes as his lips sought hers. She arched her back and buried her fingers in his shoulders.

After what seemed like eternity, Avni finally opened her eyes, still woozy from the kiss. She saw Sidharth staring at her.

He moved back, the heat rising to his face, 'Sorry, I should have asked you first.'

'What are you talking about?' she said huskily, 'That was . . . it was fine.'

'Just fine?' His voice was hoarse.

They both laughed. For both of them, it was their first kiss.

'This is the best day of my life,' Sidharth whispered in her ear.

'Mine too,' Avni replied softly.

They decided to head home.

But before Sidharth could revel in the feeling of his first kiss, something happened that made his world turn upside down. As he turned his bike towards the lane where Avni's scooty was parked, a familiar face made him stop dead in his tracks. It was his mom standing right in front of them. Avni was holding him by the waist, oblivious of his mom's presence.

Sidharth, you are so screwed today. You better come up with a plausible explanation for this or else you're doomed.

Chapter 10

Sidharth's mom was furious and was pacing the length of the living room in anger. She had always believed her son was different from the other guys but he had proven her wrong. She was like a volcano waiting to erupt. Sidharth was sitting on the sofa waiting for his mom's outburst.

'Do you have any explanation for what I saw you doing?' she asked furiously.

Sidharth was ready with his defence, 'Mom, she is just a friend. She wasn't comfortable sitting on a bike so she was holding on to me.'

Sidharth's mom was prompt to reply. 'I didn't see any kind of fear on her face. She seemed rather comfortable, if anything.'

'Mom, please stop with your assumptions.'

'Assumptions? Then what was she doing on your bike when she has her own scooty?'

Mom really needs to watch fewer crime shows. She's interrogating me like ACP Pradyuman.

'Her scooty had a flat tyre so she had asked me to drop her home. How could I leave her in college? We're neighbours. And you've only taught me to help people in times of need.'

'Don't tell me what I've said.'

Seeing no end to the discussion, Nana intervened, 'You both need to please calm down. And Anandi, if he is saying she is a friend, you should believe him. Why are you dragging things unnecessarily? Being friends with girls at his age is normal.'

'I know its normal but that girl and her family are not normal. Did you know she got two KTs in the first semester?'

'Enough, Mom. I have nothing more to say to you. If you don't believe me then there's nothing I can do to change your mind.'

Sidharth walked off in anger while his mom turned on the TV to watch another episode of her favourite crime show. It was an episode about a girl trapping a boy for money. During the entire episode, Sidharth's mom continued to imagine Sidharth and Avni as the lead actors. The episode ended with the narrator saying, *'Parents, make sure you know what your kids are up to. Sawdhan rahe, Satark rahe! Jai Hind.'*

Sidharth's mom switched off the TV and went to Sidharth's bedroom to check what he was up to. When she saw that he was taking a bath, she rummaged through his stuff looking for his mobile phone. Sidharth had left his phone to charge; she spotted it and tried to unlock it but the damn phone had a pass code. She was about to leave it when the phone buzzed with a message. It was from Avni.

'Miss you already. I hope things are fine at home. Your mom can be really scary at times.'

The message infuriated her. She sat on the bed with the phone in her hand and didn't realize when Sidharth stepped out of the washroom. He was shocked to see his mom checking his phone. He rushed to snatch it from her.

'You said she was just a friend. Then why is she sending such messages to you? "Miss you"? And how dare she call me scary?'

'You did look scary when you spotted us. I feel bad that she had to see you in that avatar.'

'Wow, so now you feel bad for her and nothing for your mother? What is this Kalyug?' She handed the phone to him. 'You will come with me to the temple tomorrow. That girl has done some black magic on you. I will take you to Guruji so he can ward off the evil.'

'Mom, I am not going anywhere. Good night.' Sidharth sighed, and asked her to leave the room.

As soon as his mother left, he called Avni,

'All good?' she asked.

'You won't believe what just happened. My mom is a complete psycho. She saw your message on my phone and has been fuming ever since.'

'Oh shit! Are you serious? WHAT THE FUCK!' It was the first time he was hearing obscenities from her mouth. It was so unlike her.

'Oh . . . so you know how to abuse as well. I've never seen you do that before,' Sidharth teased her as he noticed the panic in her voice.

'Yes, an occasional abuser. Not a serial abuser like you. So what happened?'

Sidharth narrated the entire story to her and they both burst out laughing.

'I also have to tell you something,' Avni added once they were done laughing.

'Don't tell me your parents spotted us too.'

'Actually, I told them about us during dinner, and they want to meet you tomorrow before college.'

Sidharth froze for a second. He had just escaped his mother's wrath and wasn't ready for another round of firing.

'Have you lost it? I'm not going anywhere. You could have given me some time at least. From teaming up with them in PUBG to teaming up with their daughter, things have moved really fast, as you know.'

'Just chill out,' Avni said trying to calm him down, 'They are absolutely fine with us. They aren't scary like your mother.' It was her turn to laugh.

'If my mom sees me entering your home, she will never let me enter my own house again.'

'I am sure you will manage. And aren't you a pro in PUBG? So, you should be an expert at entering the neighbouring house without letting your enemy know.' Avni continued mocking him.

Ya, funny. It's going to be solo vs squad.'

'Please, just come home.'

'Avni, please tell them that I'll meet them another time.'

'No, if you love me, then you have to come and meet them.' And with that, she hung up.

Sidharth couldn't sleep, thinking about the meeting with Avni's parents. He kept rehearsing what he would say to them. In the morning, when he got ready and was about to leave, he noticed his mom keeping a close watch on him. She hadn't got over last night's incident. Sidharth's plan to sneak into Avni's house without anyone noticing was going to be a complete failure if he couldn't come up with a plan. With no option, he took his bike to the end of the lane and parked it behind a small shop where no one could see it. He knew his mother would leave for the temple soon, and he could catch a glimpse of her from where he was standing. While he was waiting, his phone beeped.

'Where are you? They are getting late for their client meeting. Come soon.'

Sidharth felt like he was squeezed between the two families.

'Please ask them to wait. I am already in the middle of a Khatron ke Khiladi episode here.'

After waiting for almost half an hour, he saw his mother passing by. He was cautious this time to not come in her line of vision. The minute she was at a safe distance, he rushed back to their lane. He parked his bike outside and looked at himself in the mirror to make sure he looked okay.

'All the best, Sidharth,' he said to himself and rang Avni's door bell.

Soon he found himself right in front of Avni's parents.

'Will you have some coffee or will scotch do?' Avni's dad asked.

Is he joking with me? Or does he still think that I drink?

'No thanks, I don't drink, really.'

His dad came straight to the point. 'So Avni told us yesterday that you both are dating.'

Sidharth tried to explain, 'Actually ... the thing is ....'

Her dad cut him short. 'Don't worry, we are fine with you dating. In fact, we're more than fine. We've always told Avni that she should date someone in college and have a good time.'

Avni looked at Sidharth, who was sweating.

Balwinder continued, 'To be honest, you are a nice guy and brilliant in your studies. And we are glad that you both didn't hide anything from us. It would have hurt us had we found out from someone else.'

'Actually, I told Avni yesterday that she should tell you about us,' said Sidharth.

Avni couldn't believe it. Sidharth was lying! Avni's mom was quietly listening to their conversation from the kitchen while making coffee for everyone. When she returned and sat beside Balwinder, he said, 'Avni must have told you that we had a love marriage. I started dating MC when we were in our first year of college. Now I know your mother thinks you're going astray. And just like your mother, even Mona's mother was concerned about the same thing, while my parents were cool about it. I knew that trying to convince her mother would not have helped. So, instead, I focused on proving myself and, touchwood, I was able to with time. I made my career and simultaneously dated her. But I made sure to never hurt her or her parents. Never ever.'

Sidharth had got the message straight and clear. They had no objection with their relationship but wanted both Sidharth and Avni to set their priorities straight. Despite owning Jodi.com, they wanted their daughter to stand on her own feet and create her own mark in the world.

Sidharth promised him, 'I will always take care of Avni. And I will prove my merit in the days to come, I promise.'

~

Avni had read that time flies when you are with someone you love but she only realized how it felt once she got into a relationship with Sidharth. Weeks passed by like days and days like hours; from unlimited video calls to countless dates, from attending lectures to studying together, from appearing for the first year exams to going into the second year, everything passed in a blink of an eye. All this while, Avni kept telling Sidharth to stay away from the biker gang, but he continued to spend time with them. Ever so often he would get into fights started by the DK gang, much to his professors' dismay. They warned him that his internal marks would be deducted but he didn't take them seriously. He only realized that they meant what they said when the second semester results were out.

'I am not going to see the result this time. The last time I did, I got two KTs,' Bani said standing a few feet away from the notice board.

The results were put up and students rushed to the board.

'Sidharth, you should go this time. You're anyway going to top again,' Sonal suggested as she bit her nails in anxiety.

'Will you relax? Come with me,' Avni said pulling Sonal towards the board.

Sidharth waited patiently for them to come back with the results but Bani was restless. She just wanted to just get over with it.

'Your antics won't change the results, you know,' Sidharth told Bani.

'Bro, if I get a KT this time, I will kick your ass,' she replied.

'The fault is in your stars,' Sidharth teased as he borrowed a reference from one of her favourite books.

'My John Green, can you zip it for now?' said Bani.

Avni and Sonal were back with the results. Avni looked dejected.

'What happened, Chotu? Why are you sad?' Sidharth asked. He stepped closer and took her hands in his. 'But your exams had gone well. So then?'

'What's mine?' Bani interrupted Sidharth.

Sonal looked at her and said, 'Your first semester is clear. But you have got two KTs again in the second semester while I have one KT.'

'What the fuck? When will my bad luck end?'

Sidharth had eyes only for Avni. He turned her face towards him and asked, 'What's wrong?'

'She has topped the class and you're in second place,' said Sonal.

'Wow, that's amazing. So why are you upset?' When she didn't say a word, he turned towards Sonal and asked her why Avni was so upset.

'Because you could have easily got the top spot but didn't because of your low internal marks. And you know why? Because you spend all your time with DK and gang,' Sonal replied. Meanwhile, Avni left for home without Sidharth.

He called her multiple times but she kept disconnecting his calls. He waited in the balcony, but she didn't appear on the window.

Sidharth's mom was waiting for his results with bated breath.

'I stood second in class,' he said before she could ask him.

Nana congratulated him but his mother was curious to know who the first rank holder was.

'So who topped in your batch?'

Sidharth kept his bag on the table and took out a bottle of water from his bag. He took a sip and said, 'Avni. I told you she is an intelligent girl. You have the wrong perception about her.'

'My perception isn't wrong. That girl is taking advantage of you and you don't know it. She's been taking your help to study so can she get better scores than you. She was unable to clear all subjects in the first semester, and now look at her.'

'Mom, she wasn't well during the first semester. She was depressed.'

'Yes, right, I am sure she will put you in depression one day.'

Sidharth saw no point in arguing with her any further and went inside his room. Avni wasn't in the balcony; he waited for her but she didn't come. Eventually, he texted her.

Chotu, don't be angry with me. I am happier than I was when I topped.

Avni replied after a while.

First promise me that you won't hang out with those vagrants any more.

But they are my friends too, he wanted to say. *No matter how DK behaves with others, he is nice to me. And getting caught in their fights is unintentional.*

Instead, he texted a mellow response.

'Okay, I promise to stay away from them. Will you talk to me now at least?'

'I will see for a week and then I'll decide. Till then, let's be cordial with each other. But no touchy feely.'

'A week? That's too much. Also, we'll complete six months of being together next Tuesday and I want to celebrate.'

'Okay, so if you don't break your promise for a week, we celebrate.'

'What's this, yaar, you still don't believe me. I swear on you, I won't meet them.'

Avni wasn't budging and Sidharth was left with no other choice. For the rest of the week, right till Monday night, there were no late-night calls, no glances from the balconies, no lovey-dovey talks. That night when Nana was having a drink and watching the latest season of *Game of Thrones*, Sidharth came and sat next to him. He checked the time on the wall clock. It was almost 11:30 p.m. and Avni was still in no mood to listen to him. Sidharth texted her.

'If you don't say I love you and give me a kiss on the phone, I'll sneak into your house at 12 a.m. sharp.'

'Oh please. You don't have the guts.'

'Are you challenging me? And what if I take up the challenge?'

'Then you'll get whatever you want.'

Sidharth told Nana about the plan but he was a little sceptical about it.

'It's too risky. What if your mom gets up in the meantime? Can you wish her from the balcony?' Nana suggested.

'You can handle Mom. I have taken too many risks for your Old Monk. It's time to return the favour. Please. I'll be back within an hour.'

Sidharth went into his room to change and collected the gift that he had brought for her. He had framed the date of their proposal with their names written below it. He checked on his mom and once he was certain she was in deep slumber, he texted Avni. It was already midnight by then.

'Happy anniversary, Chotu. I love you in spite of our fights, our quarrels, our differences. I love you more than you will ever know. Am about to leave my house, so leave your door ajar.'

Avni was surprised that Sidharth was actually going through with his plan. Without making any noise, she tiptoed to the front door and opened it for him.

Sidharth stepped inside her gate and turned back to see if anyone as watching him. All the while, he had his heart in his mouth. He saw his grandfather in the balcony giving him a thumbs up. Avni was standing right behind the door and the minute he came inside, she closed the door hurriedly. Once inside the bedroom, Avni locked the door and Sidharth immediately hugged her.

'I can't believe you are here,' she said.

'Happy anniversary, my love,' Sidharth said pulling her cheeks.

He inched closer to her and before Avni could say anything, he sealed the moment with a passionate kiss.

'I love the way you look at me before the kiss,' she said.

'I am sorry,' said Sidharth, still holding her close to him.

'I missed you so much. I'm so sorry that I argue with you so often,' she replied returning his kiss with equal fervour.

'Its okay. Even if you do, you are my love. I'm so glad you stood first in class and I wish you would grab the top position for the next couple of years too.'

'No, I want you to be the first. You should always be on top of me.'

'Even in bed?' Sidharth asked mischievously.

'Shut up.' Avni pinched his arms and rested her head on his chest.

Sidharth hugged her tight and added in a playful tone, 'I don't mind if you are on top, even in bed. But let that be for now.'

Saying that, he pushed her on the bed. Her phone fell down from her pocket, waking a sleeping Junior. He started barking loudly. Avni rushed to him and patted him to calm him down. Just then she heard her dad calling out from his room.

'Tell Junior to stop barking. We're trying to sleep here.'

Avni was giggling, trying to control Junior. Once her father went back to sleep, Sidharth said:

'Now, it's time for another junior to wake up.'

Chapter 11

All healthy relationships go through their fair share of ups and downs. You need to have disagreements in order to know that your love is strong, that it can survive anything. Sidharth and Avni's love had not only survived but strengthened with every passing moment.

'I still remember the first day I saw you. Can you believe we're in our third year now? I was such a nerd before I met you, and how I have changed in all this time,' Avni said to Sidharth. They were sitting on the stairs of the library inside the college campus.

'These eighteen months with you have been the best days of my life. I was reckless and impatient before I met you, always taking things for granted, but your love brought stability in my life.'

'I love you so much, Sidharth. I don't think I can live without you now.' Avni kissed his hands and tightened her grip on them to show that he meant the world to her.

They had brought out the best in each other in the eighteen months of their relationship. They had learnt how to compromise for the happiness of the other person. Although Sidharth loved the company of DK and his gang, he had cut all ties with them because for him no one mattered more than Avni.

'Did you hear about the upcoming industrial visit to Chandigarh?' Bani asked as she and Sonal joined them at the stairs.

'Someone was talking about it this morning. When is it?' Sidharth asked.

'Next week. It's a five-day long trip. The charges are coming to around fifteen thousand rupees.'

'You mean this is not going to be college sponsored, and we will have to shell out the money?' Sidharth was astonished at the exorbitant price. 'And why would I go with professors and other students if I have to spend so much? I would rather take a trip to Goa with my friends.'

'What do you mean?' asked Avni.

'I mean, let's tell our parents that we are going on the industrial visit, but instead of joining the college group, we could go to Goa,' Sidharth suggested.

'Have you gone mad? That's too risky a plan,' Bani replied. With low marks and attendance, she wasn't willing to take any chances.

'Look who's talking. The girl who suggested I bring a fake dad to college in the first year.'

'No, but she is right. What if we get caught?' Avni asked.

'Trust me, nothing will happen and we will have a blast in Goa,' Sidharth assured her.

Eventually, everyone gave in. They took permission from their parents, lying about it being a college trip, and started planning their trip to Goa. Sidharth and Avni were excited about the thought of spending some much-needed alone-time at long last.

~

The Goa trip was put together by Sidharth in a matter of minutes. For a moment even he thought *'Apunich Bhagwaan hai'* and was still baffled by how everyone had agreed to his plan so easily. Anil Kapoor's dialogue was still fresh in his mind *'Aap jo keh rahe ho woh sunne ke liye achha hai, lekin practical nahi hai'*. It was only when they had boarded the train that it sunk in that they were finally going to Goa. After the train departed and they settled down, Sidharth said, 'Once we reach Goa, we will head to Candolim and look for a homestay.'

'Why a homestay? We can book a hotel,' Bani suggested.

'Darling, it's a budget trip and we cannot spend lavishly. Homestays would be cheaper and better.'

'As you say, boss,' Bani said, saluting him. 'The last time I had gone to Goa, I was in school. It was with my parents.'

'A family trip to Goa is as pointless as a bachelor party in Shirdi,' Sidharth said. 'I have checked out a few homestays on Airbnb, and have also done research on Tripadvisor for places we can visit.'

Avni's eyes sparkled with excitement, 'Awesome, I am so excited. I have never been on a trip alone with friends.'

Sonal jumped in, 'I should thank Sidharth for the transformation in you. You were hesitating to even come for the fresher's party, if you remember.'

'Why do you guys have to bring up that party every few days?' Sidharth didn't want to remember that night.

An overnight train journey with friends is always fun. They spent their time gossiping, playing games, and even irritating their fellow passengers before retiring to their respective berths. Once Bani and Sonal had drifted off to sleep, Sidharth got down from the middle berth and approached Avni, who was listening to songs on her phone.

They both chatted for a while. Then he asked, 'Can I get a kiss?' leaning closer to her.

Avni pushed him back and said, 'Shut up. Not here. Sonal or Bani may get up, and there are people around, if you haven't noticed.'

'That makes it all the more thrilling right? The fear of getting caught.'

'Don't get too naughty here. You are not going to get what you want. At least not here.'

'Is that an indication that I will get it in Goa?' Sidharth asked her hopefully.

'Put a break on your thoughts. They are running in all directions,' Avni said messing his hair by running her fingers through them.

Sidharth said, 'Everyone is sleeping. No one will come to know. Just one kiss, please.'

Avni looked around to confirm whether everyone was in deep sleep, then tilted towards him and gave him a slight peck on his lips. Her heart was racing faster than the train's speed as she moved away, sensing some movement from the lower berth. Sidharth broke into a laugh looking at her all scared, and went back to his berth with a huge smile on his face.

The train reached on time the next morning and they hired a cab to reach Candolim. After booking a homestay and relaxing in the pool for sometime, they hired a couple of Activas and explored the different beaches and forts, tried the local fish and Goan curries, did shopping and tried out a few water sports.

In the evening, they planned to go to a Baga shack and were getting ready to party. Sidharth saw Avni exit the bathroom all dressed up and her beauty took his breath away. She was wearing floral printed shorts and an off-shoulder crop top that exposed her belly button. Sidharth had never seen her in such skimpy attire.

'And then you ask me to put a break on my thoughts. How can I when you look like that?'

'You're so good with words, aren't you?' Avni pinched him.

She took his hand in hers and they left for Baga. Sonal and Bani were on one Activa and Sidharth and Avni on another. Avni was hugging him tightly, knowing she wouldn't get such chances back home.

'I love you,' she said resting her head on his shoulders. She gave him a gentle kiss on his neck.

They parked their bikes and walked towards the shore. There was loud Bollywood music playing, and they settled down in one of the shacks. They danced, partied, walked under the stars on the shore and had the time of their lives. Bani and Sonal crashed in their bedroom as soon as they returned. Avni had just come out of the shower, when Sidharth held her from behind, surprising her. He kissed her and started feeling her up when Avni pushed him.

'Pretty desperate, aren't you?' she asked.

'Yes.'

'But why? We have plenty of time.'

'How long?'

'As long as you want it,' she said, ambiguously.

Sidharth lingered for a moment on her lips before finally lifting his head to meet her eyes. He kissed her gently, carefully, but it wasn't gentleness she wanted, not today. She took him by his shirt and flung him on the bed, landing on top of him with a loud thud. He caressed her hair and nibbled at her ears. She ripped open his shirt while he took off her top. Sidharth ran his hands all over her skin. She was as soft as silk. Avni pulled him closer and buried her nails in his back.

'Someone's a little too eager,' he breathed against her neck.

Avni teased him with her fingertips as he began to stroke the length of her body with his. She moaned in pleasure. He was slow and gentle with her at first. And then they were overcome with a primal desire. Avni moaned as she felt a sharp pain. 'Shh . . . it's all right, don't worry, just relax,' he said.

She felt no more pain. Just pleasure. Incredible pleasure. Like the universe didn't exist. It was just him. And her. She didn't want the night to come to an end. Her moans got louder with each drop of sweat that tickled her skin. She held on to him as she reached the zenith of pleasure.

'I love you. Never leave me,' Avni said.

'Never. You mean everything to me,' Sidharth said and kissed her deeply. They spent the rest of the night making love to each other.

~

More than a year had passed since the Goa trip. Sidharth and Avni were no longer teenagers. But their love for each other hadn't changed. Sidharth's mother was less possessive about him now, but she still had her reservations about Avni. His nana's vision had gotten slightly blurred but his fascination for watching web series hadn't weakened. Balwinder and Mona's work pressure had increased but they still were passionate about YouTube videos and continued to address each other as MC and BC. And, for a change, Bani and Sonal had cleared all their subjects, and felt relieved at the graduation party. Students were clicking pictures at their favourite spots in college one last time.

'How times have changed,' Bani said, as they sat for one last time at their hang-out spot, 'I still remember how shit-scared we were to have one glass of alcohol during our freshers' party, and look at us now,' she said pointing to their beer cans.

Sidharth was irritated at the mention of that party. 'Four years have passed since that day but you guys won't change. I think you'll bring up the party even during my marriage, won't you?

Avni and Sonal broke into laughter. Then they all became quiet, as they thought about how life was going to change for them. There would be no more lectures, no assignments, no exams, no results and no more standing outside the xerox shop or waiting by the notice board for the results. And that, rather than making them happy, made them emotional, as they would no longer meet every day.

'So, when are you joining your new job?' Sonal asked Avni.

'Exactly a month from now.'

'Do you remember all the confusion on the placement day?' Sonal intervened.

'It was so crazy, guys,' Avni said recalling the incident. 'I had submitted my paper to the placement co-ordinator, and waited in the seminar hall for the results. After half an hour, the lady arrived with a sheet of paper and announced the names of the students who hadn't cleared the list. I was so happy that my name wasn't announced. Then the set of rejected students were announced and my name still wasn't there. Finally, I jumped when my name was announced in the selected candidates list, and I was told that I would get a call from the panel for the interview. A few minutes later, the same dumb lady came out and apologized for creating a mess. My name turned out to be on the list of the rejected candidates! I couldn't believe it. Was this a joke or something? A moment ago, she told us to wait for the call and the very next moment she said I had been rejected and would have to leave.'

'And then when we left, you got a call from HR who said he'd connect you to some interviewer. I would have beaten the shit out of him,' Sonal concluded the story.

'I wish I had done something about it that day,' Avni replied.

Avni had got placed in a company called Finolex, and had to travel to Pune for the job. Sonal had got placed in an automobile company in Mumbai. Bani was still waiting to hear back from a couple of places.

'Lucky you. I'm still without a job.'

'You should be happy that you cleared your last semester without any KT. Otherwise you would have had to repeat the year,' Sidharth teased her.

'Spare me the horror. And now, I have you to accompany me when these two go to their offices everyday.'

'Bro, I am not coming along for interviews. I opted not to join the company out of my own free will because I want to focus on raising funds for my start-up. I want to revolutionize crypto currency in India. Block chain. That's the next big thing,' Sidharth replied.

'So why did you opt for mechanical in the first place?'

'I ask myself that question every single day,' he replied.

They continued talking until Sidharth took Avni towards the parking area. He wanted to spend some time with her alone, knowing that she had to switch cities in a month. Soon they would be in a long-distance relationship. The very thought scared him. He felt miserable thinking that he could no longer gaze at her from the balcony, that they could no longer meet after college and go on long dates at the beach. Avni respected his decision to refuse the job offer from the same company in which she had been placed, but she too wasn't feeling enthused about being separated from him in the very first year of her job.

'Are you sure about your decision? You still have the offer in hand, you know. It's the highest package anyone has been offered in the mechanical branch.'

'I know. I have told Mom that I will be preparing for the MBA entrance exam but at the same time my focus would be on the idea that I have. If I can pitch it in time, I am sure I will get some angel investors on board.'

'We could have been together alone in Pune. It would have been so much fun.'

'You think I would have missed an opportunity to be alone with you? But I have to do this. For us, for our future.'

As they chatted, they didn't realize that an hour had passed. The sun had set and the farewell party was about to begin in the campus.

'Let's go. Sonal and Bani will be waiting for us.' Avni reminded him, looking at her watch.

'Not before one thing. And now I don't care about suspension either.'

He pulled her closer for a kiss. He wanted to do much more but Avni stopped him.

'I wish I could meet DK too. I haven't talked with him for a long time,' said Sidharth as they walked back towards the campus lawn.

'First, let him clear his engineering exams and pass out of college. Thank God you broke all ties with that gang.'

'It was all for you.'

When they reached, the music was on full blast. Bani and Sonal were grooving on the dance floor. Avni joined them, dragging Sidharth with her. Sidharth couldn't believe how a girl who was so reserved in the first year of college had transformed into this carefree girl.

Avni closed her eyes and let the music wash over her. The music echoed the sound of her life and her feet were like the raging waters of a waterfall, swift and vibrant and full of energy, like never before. The second she started moving, the slight jitters that she had melted in the joint swells of music and pleasure. Her heartbeat accelerated and she stood with her back arched and her hands stretched to the sky as if in submission. The lights were bright and the rhythm started to pulse in her.

She tapped her feet to the steady beat. Back and forth, she swayed as the beat picked up pace. Even Bani and Sonal joined her.

Sidharth was in awe of her and stood watching her dance. Her eyes were shining, and her lips kissed the threshold of liberty as she danced her inhibitions away. Her elbows gracefully moved through the air, which traced a curve that no menace could surpass. Her waist undulated vivaciously seeming to reject all the silent judgements that the world offered to her all this while. There was nothing that could calm her tempestuous spirit. Sidharth saw a changed Avni; her confidence had grown gradually, and he hadn't noticed it until that day. Like a mermaid would break through the surface of the water, she broke through all the limitations that she had imposed on herself all these years.

And when the track changed into a slow romantic one, Bani and Sonal pushed Sidharth onto the dance floor. She felt right in his arms as they swayed gently to the song.

'Tell me you'll love me forever,' she whispered in his ear.

'I'll love you till the last breath.'

Avni smiled and hugged Sidharth. Suddenly Sidharth started to feel dizzy and his feet gave way.

'Are you okay? Do you want some water?' Avni asked as she tried to hold him upright.

His vision was blurred and speech slurry. Sidharth couldn't understand what was happening to him and before he knew it, he had collapsed on the floor.

'Sidharth . . . please open your eyes . . .' she kept screaming in shock, shaking him with the hope that he would get up. She prayed that it was a prank and that he would get up the next moment. But he didn't. He was fine a moment ago and then he was on the ground, unconscious. Sonal, Bani and a few students rushed to him to take him to the hospital. His mother was informed immediately, and she and his nana hurried to the hospital.

Avni was crying uncontrollably when they reached. The reports had come and the doctor called his family inside the room. Sidharth had insisted that the doctors read the report in his presence. The glass window separated Avni from Sidharth, but she could clearly see the fear in everyone's eyes. She wanted to know what had happened to him, she wanted to be there beside him, hold his hand and tell him not to worry. She wanted to caress his forehead and tell him that everything would be fine. She hoped and prayed it wasn't anything serious.

'I'm afraid I don't have good news for you,' the doctor told the family. 'He's got a brain tumour. And we need to start his treatment immediately. There's very little time left.'

Sidharth and his family were shocked to hear this, but he remained calm, knowing Avni was watching him from outside. He looked at her and smiled, gesturing that he was fine. But only he knew that his smile hid an unfathomable grief. Avni had just started to feel better, and he didn't want her to go back into her shell again. She wouldn't be able to survive another setback, so he thought it best to keep the information to himself for now.

Chapter 12

I *am in a constant state of turmoil every day. How could this be happening to me? I feel so weak—both physically and mentally.*

Ever since his shocking diagnosis, Sidharth had begun to make notes in his diary—it kept him distracted from his condition. Avni was still in the dark about it and was told that he was just weak. He was undergoing a tsunami of emotions trying to detach himself from her.

When the doctors told me I have a tumour, I didn't know how to react. Until then I had thought I was healthy and strong but I was so wrong. Every day feels like a losing battle. My treatment will start soon but I'm not feeling very hopeful. The doctors wanted to start immediately but I needed time to steady myself. I have been avoiding Avni for the last few days. I know she'll be pissed with me for keeping the truth from her. But how can I tell her? She has barely overcome the loss of a loved one. If anything were to happen to me, I know she will not be able to bear it. And after she finds out, I won't be able to take care of her because this damn tumour is emotionally draining me. She is leaving next week for Pune and I have no clue how to face her.

He shut his diary and was about to take a shower when he received a call from Avni. He had been avoiding her like the plague and she knew something was up with him.

He finally picked up on the fourth ring, 'Why are you avoiding me?' she asked.

'I am not. I was going for a shower,' Sidharth lied.

'Is it? Then come to the balcony. I want to see how dirty you look.'

Sidharth knew Avni would catch his lie.

'Not now. I am just headed inside.'

After a long silence from Avni, she asked in a heartbreaking tone, 'What's wrong, Sidharth? You haven't been yourself since our graduation day and the trip to the hospital. Is anything the matter? Everything was going well and you've suddenly cut off all ties from me. I miss you, Sidharth. You know you can tell me anything, right?'

Do you know how it feels to hide the biggest truth of my life from the person I love the most in the world? Do you know how it feels to love you and still stay detached? Do you know how I would feel when you will come to know the truth and break down?

'Will you please tell me?' Avni kept insisting.

'Nothing is wrong; please believe me. It's just that the anxiety of you going away from me that's making me sick. Let's meet tomorrow and I promise I'll be the same Sidharth as before.'

After a quick bath, he went and sat outside with his nana. Ever since his diagnosis, his nana had given up watching TV or drinking. Sidharth made him a drink, took the glass and sat beside him.

'Here,' he said handing him the glass.

'I don't feel like it,' his grandfather said glumly.

'Have it for me. I know you are sad, but I can't see you like this.'

'And do you think I can see you like this? How can life be so cruel? It would have been better had I got it. I've lived a full life,' his nana lamented.

Sidharth held his grandfather's hands to comfort him, and said, 'Don't worry, I will be fine soon. And who will get you more alcohol on the sly if I go, right?'

His nana starting sobbing like a little child. He couldn't believe Sidharth at his age could be so pragmatic, so hopeful, so full of life. Nana realized he had to be strong for his grandchild. He wiped his tears and assured him everything would be fine and that he would come out of it a champion. 'Sidharth, can I ask you one thing? Why are you running away from Avni? I have seen how both of you are each other's emotional support. I think you should tell her. She is stronger than you think.'

'Nana, I really love her and my heart aches at the thought of not being with her. I know it's just a passing phase and I will recover from this. But till this phase ends, I cannot be with her. She'll immediately know that something is wrong. And I don't want her to suffer the way she did when her nani passed away. She won't be able to face another trauma. If there is one person she is emotionally attached to after her nani, it's me.'

'What if your recovery takes time? How long can you keep this a secret from her?'

'I have no choice. I know what I am doing is wrong but sometimes you have to do what's wrong to protect the person you love.' He took Nana's hand and kept it on his head. 'Promise me that you won't ever tell her. Not until I tell you to.'

'I promise,' he said fighting back tears. He muttered a silent prayer to the almighty.

Please give strength to these kids.

Sidharth's mom was eavesdropping on their conversation. She didn't intervene, and cried silently. She had been devastated ever since the news was broken to her. All her beliefs and assumptions about the world had shattered in that moment.

~

'Sidharth, will you miss me when am gone?' Avni asked.

They had driven to Nariman Point to spend some time together. Seeing the couples around them, Sidharth wished everything could get back to how it was before. He would have been sitting with her, hand in hand. He would have hugged her, kissed her and felt her warmth on his skin without worrying about the people around them. He was meeting her after a long time and he wanted to make her feel special. He had got her bunch of red roses and Avni's face lit up when he gave them to her. Sidharth kept looking at the glow in her eyes and realized just how much he had missed her all these days.

'Don't stare at me that way. You're making me nervous,' she said turning red in the face.

Sidharth smiled. He kissed her cheeks and hugged her as tightly as he could, not wanting to let her go just yet.

'Can I tell you one thing?' Avni asked still enveloped in the hug.

'Ya,' Sidharth said, breathing in the scent of her body.

'These last few days have made me realize that I cannot live without you. I love you and think about you all the time. I really don't know what's going on inside your head, but please don't ever think of leaving me. You are my lifeline.'

Avni had missed him so much these last few days; it was killing her to not be able to text him and talk to him. Just hearing his voice on the phone was enough to melt her heart. Sidharth thought of telling her the truth, but stopped himself. He didn't have the strength to see her in pain. They spent the entire evening in each other's arms, gazing at the endless sea. Once they reached home, Avni texted Sidharth before going to bed.

I promise to love you for all the years we will have together. I cannot imagine a day without you by my side. You are the person who gives meaning to my life. You are my forever. You make me so, so happy. Don't ever think of leaving me because I have no existence without you.

Sidharth sent her a kissing emoji. He had decided that he would not meet Avni on the day she left Mumbai. He didn't want to end the day by upsetting her again but he knew this decision was definitely going to hurt her. On the day of her departure, Avni messaged Sidharth.

'Where are you? Come home, I am waiting for you. I have sent both Mom and Dad out to buy a few essential things for me. They won't be coming back for at least an hour. So, we have that time all for ourselves.'

Avni sent a naughty GIF along with the message and kept the phone aside as she went back to packing her stuff. A few minutes later, the phone beeped with a message from Sidharth.

Avni, I didn't want to tell you yesterday but I will not be able to see you off. I can't see you leaving. I love you and once you're settled, I'll will come to Pune to meet you. But not today. Happy journey, my Chotu.

Avni was startled to read such a message from Sidharth. She called him back immediately but he didn't pick up.

'Please pick up my call. Don't do this to me.'

But Sidharth neither replied nor picked up her calls. She left everything aside and decided to go to his house. She latched the door and had just stepped outside when she saw her parents coming back. Seeing her sobbing, her mom asked, 'What happened? Is everything fine?'

'Yes and no. You guys go home, please. I'll be back in some time.'

'But why are you—' But before her mom could finish, Avni had gone.

'Don't worry. She might have picked up a fight with Sidharth. She'll be fine. We'll talk once she's back,' said Balwinder.

Avni rang Sidharth's doorbell, still in tears. His mother opened the door. Seeing Avni cry, she asked her to come inside.

'Beta, what happened? Why are you crying?' she asked.

'Aunty, where is Sidharth? I want to meet him.' Avni sobbed.

'He's not at home. Why don't you call him and ask?' she said, and made her sit. 'I'll bring some water for you.'

'He isn't taking my calls. He's not even replying to my messages. I am leaving in an hour for Pune, and I want to meet him before I leave.'

Till that day, Sidharth's mother had never really supported their relationship, but at that moment, she felt how wrong she was in judging Avni.

I always thought Avni wasn't the right girl for him and that she would destroy my son's life. How wrong I was. I know today that its only her love that can pull Sidharth out from his present state of misery. I need to tell her the truth before it's too late, even if it means I'm going against Sidharth's wish.

She took a deep breath and said, 'I am sorry for not supporting your relationship since the beginning. I'm sorry for doubting you. But today, I know that your love for him is true. And I have to tell you what Sidharth has kept hidden from you for the last one month.'

'What is it?' Avni whispered, dreading what she was going to hear.

Sidharth's mother had always asked Sidharth to stay away from Avni but today, the intense love in her eyes melted her heart. She told Avni the whole truth. Avni felt a sense of numbness. She couldn't think clearly. Everything around her was a haze. Sidharth's mother shook her to bring her back to her senses.

'He has gone out with his grandfather. But they didn't tell me where they were going.'

'I know where they might be. I'll go meet him.'

Avni rushed to the Happy Club. She knew that was the only place where he would go with his nana. That was the only place where he could find some sense of solace and happiness. And she wasn't wrong. He was there with Mr Wagle and his grandfather.

Sidharth was surprised to see Avni standing at the entrance. Tears filled his eyes. He had thought he would not see her anytime soon. The emotion in his eyes expressed everything that Sidharth couldn't in the past one month. Avni saw him fight back his tears and rushed towards him.

'Who told you I was here? You were supposed to leave today, right?'

'Why couldn't you just tell me, Sidharth? You think our love is so weak? I found out everything from your mom.'

Sidharth's legs gave way and he fell on the floor. He buried his face in his hands and said, 'I am sorry, please forgive me.'

Avni pulled him up. 'I know you're probably feeling scared and overwhelmed right now. You're scared because you don't know what the future holds for us and because you think I won't be able to take this news. You're wrong, Sidharth. You've always been the one to carry my burden and now it is my turn. I will not let you go through this journey alone. I know that you will be strong throughout your battle, but I also want to tell you that you don't have to be strong. When you are afraid or angry, you don't have to hide that from me. We will fight this together. I love you so much.'

'I thought you wouldn't be able to handle it.'

Avni placed her finger on his lips and said, 'If you can be my strength, then can't I be yours? Relationships will be put to the test, and may change. We should remember that this isn't all about us. It's about those closest to you, too, and sometimes it can be more than they can bear. You'll have to be the strong one for them!'

Avni promised that she would never let her pillar of strength fall.

Chapter 13

One minute your life is perfect, and the very next minute everything around you can come crashing down. But Sidharth wasn't alone in his fight now. Both his and Avni's family gave him enough hope and encouragement to fight through his treatment and come out a winner. With not much to do, Sidharth started penning down his thoughts daily in his diary. It not only helped him divert his mind from the tremendous pain but also gave him hope that there was light at the end of this dark tunnel.

I was devastated when Avni came to know about my condition. I thought she would not be able to bear the news. But today she is my biggest strength and support.

It's so strange to think that the thing that can make you dangerously sick or even kill you is in you. It just sits there.

Deep inside your body, waiting to someday take hold of your life. It's hard for me to wrap my brain around this. That I can have something waiting, sitting dormant inside me. It scares me but if there's one thing I'm really afraid of, it's chemotherapy. Every session of chemo causes me several side effects. I get headaches and shooting pain in my hands and legs. My mouth feels sore and my stomach is all knotted up. How will I continue to cope with it? But my family and Avni's family have been my biggest pillars of strength during this time. They make me feel like I can overcome even bigger challenges than this. All these years, I wasn't successful in breaking the wall of discomfort between my mom and Avni. The tumour made it possible. She praises Avni the whole day, seeing the kind of effort she puts to keep me balanced. That always makes me smile. Almost every day I have nausea and fatigue but whenever I see them together, it gives me joy.

I am surrounded by people who constantly make jokes and keep me smiling. I've spent a total of six weeks at the hospital, receiving rounds of chemo on a weekly basis. And every chemo session breaks me a little. The very thought of chemo shakes me to my core. I've tried every stunt and excuse to avoid chemo. In the end, I always end up in the chair watching that green concoction slowly flow into my body. The next morning my body is filled with pain. Even painkillers can't numb the pain. Each day is a battle to survive. I've been moody and irritable, but Avni has stayed calm and patient throughout.

He put down his pen and looked at Avni, who was monitoring his stats. 'Is your job offer still valid? If so, I think you should accept it. How many days and months will you continue to waste on me, doing nothing?' Sidharth asked. 'I don't know if the tumour is shrinking. The doctors haven't told me anything.

'I'll wait for as long as it takes.'

'But I don't want . . .'

'Look, I don't want any suggestions from you. And it's not like I'm sitting here doing nothing. I am preparing for my MBA entrance on the side. Plus I am learning the work of Jodi.com, and helping your mom in all the household chores. And that isn't less than any internship. And taking care of you, that's something I can do tirelessly.'

She tried to make him smile but it was one of those days when he was feeling low.

'Your life would be so much simpler if you were with someone else; someone without a debilitating illness like mine.'

'I don't care if you recover or not. I am not leaving your side. Even if given a chance, I wouldn't want to be with anyone else. When I look at you, I don't see a person held captive by his tumour. No, I see a hero, I see someone who embodies strength, character and endurance. I see a winner.' Sidharth knew she could be really stubborn when she wanted to.

About a month later, I was finally home after the completion of stage 1 of my treatment. Weekly infusions of chemo became bi-monthly infusions. A lot had changed about me since I had first started taking treatment. I had learned how to live with pain. It had become the one constant in my life. I took fewer painkillers than I did before because I had grown comfortable with that feeling. I had a new outlook on life and I no longer let it stop me from doing things that I had done before my treatment. Due to the amount of chemotherapy I was undergoing, my immune system had been destroyed. This meant that one simple germ could cost me my life. Thus I could not be roaming freely with anyone and everyone. I still had my fun though, for Avni, my mom, Nana and Avni's parents always found a way to keep the mood light.

Avni's dad would refer to PUBG in their conversations, 'Don't worry, you will not only survive the last zone but will grab a chicken dinner at the end of it.'

They always kept me entertained even though I never managed to get more kills than him. Whether it was corny jokes, camping in the living room, or movie nights, we were always finding ways to have fun. Their videos entertained me whenever I felt depressed and, recently, they had started making inspiring videos to keep me motivated. Had it not been for their positive and uplifting attitude, I wouldn't have stayed strong.

It wasn't just about the mental strength; physically, too, I was a challenge. I had lost a lot of weight after the first treatment. People had told me horror stories about chemotherapy and all of it was coming true for me. I felt good that I didn't lose my hair. But after the first few rounds of chemo, I was taking a shower and shampooing my hair. The next thing I knew, I was holding the biggest bunch of hair in my fist. I felt horrible. My mom shaved my hair the next morning and I spent almost a week avoiding the mirror. The worst part was that even Junior didn't recognize me until Avni convinced him that it was really me. Avni told me I looked more macho in my bald state but I know she was just encouraging me.

'I don't care about your looks. I don't care whether you are bald or you have hair. I don't care about what tumour you have. I don't care about what the future holds. I don't care about any of that. But what I do know is that I love you. I know that God has a bigger plan for us. That there's a bigger purpose for this suffering. I know that one day, this whole mess is going to be okay. I have faith in Him. And I'm not going to worry about what I can't control.'

She kissed my cheeks. I was speechless. We were strong before, but even stronger now.

As weeks turned into months, I continued to fight for my life. Seven months from the date of my first therapy, I underwent an operation. The doctors were successful in removing the tumour. I had put everything that I had into my recovery and into staying healthy and germ-free.

A couple of days after the operation, his mother came and sat beside him. 'The doctors say that you have responded to the treatment brilliantly, and soon, you will be back to your normal self.'

'Yes, and we'll have a drink together,' chimed in his nana, much to the dismay of his daughter. But he didn't care. His grandson was recovering and nothing mattered more to him.

Avni had a triumphant smile on her face as she saw the interaction between them. All she wanted to do was hug and kiss him once he was back home after the surgery, safe and healthy.

'See, I had told you that you will come out a winner. I am so proud of you,' she said.

In the last seven months, my tumour made me see what truly mattered the most, and made me think differently about how the drama, pettiness and the inconsequential stuff that suck away too much of our attention, are just not important. It made me incredibly aware of one thing—time. There are no guarantees, we can't relive yesterday or live tomorrow; all we really have is right now, this moment, and I learned to make the most out of every second of it.

With every passing day, Sidharth's health kept getting better. But he still hadn't recovered completely and was emotionally weak. Once he was discharged, the doctors suggested he go on a short vacation as the change of place would do him good. Avni's parents were supposed to go to Shimla to attend a destination wedding arranged by Jodi.com. Since Avni had worked on the project, she asked her parents if she could go instead of them, taking Sidharth with her. They were elated at the idea. Avni was determined to make this mini vacation one of the best ones of Sidharth's life.

~

'So, we are finally here!' Avni said after completing the check-in formalities at the hotel. They were in Shimla, at a beautiful hotel located on a hilltop, with a magnificent view of the Himalayas.

Looking at her as she unpacked their clothes and laid them on the bed, Sidharth kept wondering what gave her so much hope and strength during his worst phase. Not even once had she looked fragile since the day she got to know about Sidharth. Avni took a file out of her bag and walked towards Sidharth. She kissed him on his forehead and said, 'The groom's uncle is in the lobby. I will just finish some work and then we will have the entire day to ourselves. Until then, plan something exciting.'

After Avni left, Sidharth went to the washroom to take a bath. He freshened up and came out only in a towel. He was drying himself when the doorbell rang. He thought it was Avni and went to open the door.

In all his excitement, he didn't even bother looking through the keyhole to make sure it was her. As soon as the door opened and a woman entered, he leapt at her and she screamed. To Sidharth's utter shock, he realized it was the staff lady who had come in to leave some bottles of water in their room. *Shit, I forgot to leave the Do Not Disturb sign on the door!* He let her free, apologizing for his mistake. The lady was visibly shaken.

'I am really sorry. I didn't expect you at the door.'

'It's okay. I understand.' She walked out of the room as quickly as she could. Sidharth then noticed Avni standing by the door, laughing.

Sidharth pulled her to him, hugging her tightly. 'My baby got scared?' Avni said, kissing him.

'Maybe I should have let her kiss me too,' he teased.

'Shut up. You are just mine.' Avni pulled his cheeks and went inside the washroom to change. Sidharth got dressed in the meanwhile and googled places to visit nearby. He had regained his confidence and could look in the mirror now; the hope to live had been reignited in his soul, and it was all because of Avni's support. When she came out, she was happy to see Sidharth looking all dapper.

'It's so good to see you like this, Mr Handsome. I love you so much.'

Sidharth cupped her face and said, 'I don't know what to say. You loved me when I least deserved it. You are so special to me, my Chotu.'

Both Sidharth and Avni were twinning in red sweaters. After clicking a few photographs in the room, they got a call from the reception that their car was ready. Sidharth had booked a cab for Kufri. He had planned to take her for a candlelight dinner at a restaurant, and had booked a table with a breathtaking view of the snow-capped mountains and the star-studded sky. When they reached, the manager welcomed them and escorted them to their table.

'I love these little surprises that you plan. And with you by my side, everything becomes magical.' Avni said as they walked towards the table he had reserved.

'This is just a small token of my appreciation for all the things you have done.'

'I am not done yet,' Avni smiled.

'What do you mean?'

'I mean that I'll keep caring for you till my last breath. But that's possible only if you say yes.'

'Yes? For what?'

'To marry me, you idiot.' She paused and gazed into his eyes, and then said, 'I want to marry you. I want to be yours forever.'

Before Sidharth could say anything, Avni sealed the moment with a kiss. The girl who once felt embarrassed when her parents displayed their affection in public, was today sailing on the same ship of love. Sidharth was hesitant initially but couldn't control his urge, and the anxiety about his health was burned down by the passion and warmth of her touch.

After dinner, the cab dropped them a short distance from the hotel. They walked in the hotel's direction, clinging on to each other for warmth. Sidharth still hadn't said a formal yes to her proposal. Avni knew why he was sceptical. But she had made up her mind. The next day during the marriage function, she had planned something special for him.

~

As the wedding ceremonies unfolded the next day, the groom's dad came to Avni and said, 'You guys have done a fantastic job. I still remember how cynical we were to meet the bride's family as they belonged to another caste. But you and your team have been amazing at making sure our families gel well and that we are the right fit for each other.'

'Thank you, Uncle. We wish the groom and bride all the happiness.' Avni smiled, breathing a sigh of relief.

He patted Sidharth on the back and left. Sidharth looked towards Avni and said, 'I am so proud of you, Chotu. This was your first assignment and you've done a fab job.'

'The next one will be ours,' Avni winked.

Later, when Avni watched the bride arrive, she was transported into a dream world. She imagined herself wearing a beautiful bridal outfit, walking towards the mandap, as everyone stared at her in awe. She visualized Sidharth making promises to love her, to keep her safe and happy until the end of his days. She saw Sidharth sliding a small ring on her finger and her doing the same to him. Engraved on the rings was the word 'Forever'. Then Sidharth would pull out the mangal sutra and place it around her neck. 'You are officially mine now,' he would whisper to her.

They would kiss in front of the guests, who would then break into applause.

She was brought back to reality when she heard her name being announced. The groom's father had finished with his speech and, at the end of it, he called Avni on the stage to give her a gift as a token of their appreciation.

'You know, I was just dreaming that we were getting married and you kissed me in front of all the guests.' She winked and walked towards the stage. Sidharth laughed at her crazy thought. Once Avni took the stage, the groom's father said, 'She is the person who made this event successful and I would like everyone to give her a huge round of applause.'

Once Avni had accepted his gift, she asked him, 'Can I say a few words?'

The groom's father assumed she wanted to give her best wishes to the newly weds, and handed over the mike to her.

'I would like to congratulate both the families on this auspicious occasion. As the rituals were being conducted, I couldn't help but visualize my love, Sidharth, and I, in the place of the bride and the groom. There he is . . .' Avni said pointing towards him. All the guests turned in his direction. *Where is this speech going?* Sidharth wondered.

'It's been more than four years since we first met. The memory of it is still fresh in my mind and every time I think about it, a small smile escapes my lips. We hear people say often, 'You'll know when the person you have in front of you is THE ONE . . . its funny but it's true. Since you've come into my life, nothing has mattered to me more than your presence. Together we have gone through so much. You pulled me out of my depression, and I was there by your side when you were battling with your health. We won both battles because of our support for each other. But now I know that I want this support for a lifetime. I want to marry you. I want to be your wife. I want you to be the first person I see when I wake up. I want to lie next you and snuggle every night. I want you to share your dreams and your fears, your likes and your dislikes, the things that you love and those that you hate. And I want to take them and make them mine. I love you, Sidharth. Will you marry me?'

Sidharth was overwhelmed, and all the while Avni expressed her feelings, he had images of them getting married. He had dreamt about it countless times since the day he had fallen for Avni. How many times he had imagined her in a red bridal dress, walking towards him and holding his hand, announcing to the world that they were made for each other. Even at that moment, he was lost in these thoughts, and all the fear that had engulfed him since last night vanished. He couldn't decline her proposal. She stepped down from the stage as he ran towards her and enveloped her in a tight hug. He kissed her in front of all the guests. 'Yes, a thousand times yes,' he repeated, as the guests rose form their seats and hooted for them. Two flames that had endured the strongest of storms were united to survive a thousand more. Together they found comfort. Clocks no longer counting minutes, but every moment timeless.

Chapter 14

A Few Years Later

It had been a few years since Sidharth and Avni's marriage. Sidharth had become stronger and regained his health, all thanks to Avni. Within a month of their marriage, Sidharth got the funding for his dream start-up, and he believed Avni was his lucky charm. Avni too had joined an automobile company while continuing to work with her parents on Jodi.com.

Sidharth's medical check-ups continued for the next few months and although he had overcome the worst, the doctors had asked him to take extra care of his health and not take too much stress at work. Avni ensured everything was well taken care of. She had transitioned from girlfriend to wife with ease.

Sidharth and Avni had a son two years after marriage. They named their son 'Shivaansh.'

It was the day of his first birthday. 'Can you believe our baby boy is one already?' Sidharth asked, pulling his son's cheeks as Avni cradled him in her arms.

She smiled back at him and said, 'I know, I can't believe it either.'

They were in their bedroom getting ready for the party. Avni wanted to get ready so Sidharth took Shivaansh in his arms.

'Come to Daddy,' he said tickling him. Avni went to take a bath as Sidharth laid Shivaansh on the bed and started showing him his new toys. After a few minutes, he suddenly started crying, and Sidharth realized that he had pooped.

'Oh damn, Shivaansh, why do you always have to poop when Mummy is not around?' Just then, Avni walked out of the washroom.

'He smells horrible. Avni, you're changing him, not me!' Sidharth said covering his nose with his sleeve.

'No way. I just had a bath. And I changed him in the afternoon. So it's your turn now.'

'What's this, yaar. Can't he give us some sign before he poops?'

'Ya, develop AI for that too,' Avni laughed looking at Sidharth's expression.

He took him to the washroom begrudgingly and changed his diaper, gave him a bath, and got him dressed in his birthday outfit. They had made him wear an Iron Man suit, and he looked really adorable in it.

'I'll go and have a bath now, again. I smell like shit, literally,' Sidharth said making a face.

'Its been a year now, you should get used to diaper duties, Daddy,' Avni teased him.

'Shut up and give me a kiss right now,' Sidharth pulled Avni into his arms.

'No way, go clean yourself first. Dirty Daddy.' She pushed him into the washroom.

She took Shivaansh in her arms and went outside. Sidharth's mother was bringing the cake to the living room, which was decorated with balloons and ribbons. Avni helped her in the preparations. They had become very close since her marriage and now they shared a beautiful relationship.

'Where's Sidharth? He isn't ready yet?' she asked.

'Mummy, he was ready, but I guess Shivaansh didn't like his look because he pooped on him,' Avni laughed, and his mother joined in the laughter.

'Now he'll understand what it's like to be a parent,' she said and picked Shivaansh in her arms, 'Happy birthday, my little Sidharth.'

'Are you guys celebrating alone?' Sidharth's nana jumped in. 'Where is Chadha Saab?' he asked Avni, looking at his watch.

'I just had a word with them, they are just leaving the house,' Avni said.

'We are already here. This MC takes a lot of time to do her make up. She forgets that she is now a nani and not a young lady any more,' Balwinder said as he walked in bearing gifts.

'Oh yes, that's why my solo videos garner more views than yours, you old man,' she replied.

So much had changed over the years but not Balwinder and Mona. They were still experts in pulling each other's leg. Nana had got Balwinder addicted to *Game of Thrones*, much to Mona's dismay. Sidharth's mother felt content looking at her new extended family. For once, she was proud of her son and his choice.

Once Sidharth joined them in the living room, Avni put the cake on the table, holding Shivaansh in her arms. Everyone burst into a happy birthday song as Sidharth and Avni blew out the candles. Avni cut a slice of the cake and fed a tiny slice to Shivaansh. He took the slice in his hand and smeared his face with it, making everyone laugh.

'He's so cute,' Mona said, and took a picture of them. Sidharth's grandfather opened a bottle of champagne as slices of cake were handed out. After a session of drinks and dinner at the end of the day, Avni's mom kissed her forehead and said, 'I am so proud of you two. You were just kids when you started dating, and look at you guys now! You even have a baby boy who's just turned a year old. I still can't believe it sometimes. God has been kind.' Tears ran down her cheeks. Avni embraced her mother.

'I love you both so much,' she said.

At night, when Sidharth and Avni were alone in the room, with Shivaansh sleeping between them, Sidharth looked into Avni's eyes. They radiated the same intensity of love that he had felt during their college days. Avni looked at Shivaansh and said affectionately, 'He is going to be as handsome as his dad when he grows up.'

Sidharth stroked her cheek. 'And I can only hope our boy finds someone just like you to anchor his life.'

He kissed her hand and they cuddled passionately. Love is a short word, easy to spell, difficult to define and impossible to live without. Every moment they spent together had touched their lives, their souls forever. It seemed like the perfect ending to their story.

But fate had other plans for them. A few months later, Sidharth started to feel bouts of pain in his body. It got so bad that he was finding it difficult to even walk, and that's when Avni found out. He had tried his best to keep it hidden from her but he couldn't keep it a secret any longer. Though he resisted going to a doctor at first, Avni wasn't going to take any chances. They scheduled a visit to the same doctor who had treated him earlier. He was sent for a couple of tests and put under observation. Both the families waited for the results to come in. The fear was evident on their faces. They hoped and prayed that everything was normal.

When the doctor called them to his room, he showed them the reports. 'I'm sorry I don't have very good news. We're seeing a tumour recurrence, in medical terms. We will need to treat it as soon as possible.'

Avni was heartbroken at those words. 'Can it be cured totally?'

'We cannot say anything at this moment. But we will try our best.'

Avni was unable to speak. Sidharth's grandfather was in tears.

'Shri Krishna, Shri Krishna . . .' Sidharth's mother began chanting, praying for her son's recovery.

'Oh God, you have been with us through all the rough times. Please, one more time, be with us. I need him, Shivaansh needs him. We all need him.' Avni prayed as she observed Sidharth from outside his room. No one was allowed to enter the room.

For the next few days, Sidharth would be kept under observation at the hospital. With nothing left for them to do except pray, they left for home, feeling miserable.

Avni tried hard to keep negative thoughts at bay, but they kept haunting her. She would look at Shivaansh's face whenever she felt low, and start to cry. Every evening his mother would do a puja at home while his nana took to chanting 'OM' with the help of Rudraksh beads. Avni tried to put up a brave front for his mother and nana, cracking jokes and making them smile whenever she could.

Each one of them took turns visiting Sidharth at the hospital since only one person was allowed to be with him at a time. The days were pretty much the same, with no improvement in his condition. On the fourth day, when Avni reached the hospital with a basket of fruits, she saw Sidharth's nana and her dad discussing something with the doctor. The serious look on their faces told her it wasn't good news. She rushed towards them but, by the time she reached, the doctor had left. She saw how sleepy her dad looked. He had been awake all night keeping a watch on Sidharth. 'What did the doctor say?' asked Avni.

'That he is responding to treatment. But it's still too early to say anything. They are figuring out the best time to operate on him.'

'He'll be fine soon,' Sidharth's nana added.

Their comforting words made Avni feel better. She had been worried sick about him and this news was like a small ray of hope for her, as Sidharth's health had been deteriorating daily. A smile appeared on her face and she asked, 'How's Sidharth? Is he feeling better?'

'Yes, he had breakfast in the morning and has been watching television ever since. But he keeps looking at his watch. I think he's waiting for you,' her dad beamed.

Avni kissed her dad on the cheek and asked him and Nana to go home and get some rest.

'Nanaji, you've been here since last night and you must be tired. Please go home and relax. I'll be back in the evening before Mom comes. I will give your legs my special Ayurvedic massage.'

Sidharth's nana patted her shoulder and left with Avni's dad. Avni took a deep breath and stepped inside the room. She hated to see Sidharth lying seemingly lifeless on the bed. All she wanted was to take him home. Sidharth opened his eyes and saw Avni placing the fruit basket on the table.

'Shivaansh?' Sidharth asked as he tried to sit up.

'No, don't get up,' Avni said rushing to him and adjusting his pillow. 'I left Shivaansh with Mom. He's been crying since the morning, and bringing him here would have made him all the more restless,' she replied.

'I wanted to see him,' Sidharth said in a dejected tone.

'I will tell Mom to bring him in the evening.' Avni assured him and kissed his forehead.

She kept looking at him.

'Why are you looking at me like that? I'm fine.' He saw how worried she looked. He didn't want Avni to feel his pain and tried hard to pretend that he was okay.

Sidharth was pale. Avni knew her dad was just comforting her, for his condition hadn't got any better. She took his hand. It was cold and he had no strength to grip her hand. She felt terrible. She remembered all those times in bed when they would cuddle, their fingers intertwined. Those memories brought tears to her eyes, and a tear fell on Sidharth's hand. She avoided looking at him to hide her tears but couldn't. Sidharth lifted her head up with his hands and said, 'You have to be strong, for me and for Shivaansh. And I am not dying anytime soon. Stop worrying so much.'

Avni sealed his lips with her finger. 'Don't you dare say such a thing again. I will not let anything happen to you. Death has to cross me first before it reaches you. And I am a tough girl. So, stop with your idiotic thoughts.'

'You know, last night I dreamt that I had recovered, and we have gone to Paris together. We were sitting under the Eiffel Tower and I was kissing you passionately.'

'You're mad! How can you be having such wild dreams in the hospital?'

'What can be better than dreaming about you? There's nothing in this world that matches my love for you,' he said as Avni blushed. He kissed her hand. 'No matter what the future holds, no matter what the doctors say, nothing can tear us apart. Not even the devil. A part of me will always be you and a part of you will always be me.'

'I love you forever. For better or for worse,' she said, hugging him.

They spent the entire afternoon talking and reminiscing about the past. In the evening, when his mother came, he expected to see Shivaansh with her but she had left him at home with his nana as he was sleeping.

'Don't worry, I'll get him tomorrow. I am leaving now but just call me if you feel like talking to me. It's just a matter of a few hours. I'll see you tomorrow; love you so much. And wait for tomorrow. I have a surprise for you,' said Avni.

'What's that? Tell me now. I can't wait till tomorrow.'

'Don't act like a kid, you are a father now.' Avni teased him.

On her way back in a cab, Avni was looking out of the window, thinking about them, when she suddenly felt Sidharth's presence. She felt like he was sitting beside her, playing with her hair and touching her skin. She was tired and sleepy and maybe her mind was playing games with her. She shut her eyes, hoping Sidharth would disappear. But when she looked again, she saw Sidharth sitting beside her.

This can't be real.

But there he was. And the more she saw him, the more real he felt. There were no tubes around him and he looked like his usual boyish self.

'Can you give me my surprise now?' he asked. 'I have come especially for that.'

'Didn't I tell you that I would give it to you tomorrow?'

'Why? I need it now.'

'That's not fair.'

'Everything is fair when it comes to surprises.'

Avni had written him a letter, just like he had many years ago.

She handed over the letter to him and kissed him.

Before he could read the letter, she snatched it away from his hands. 'Now what?'

'Tomorrow.'

'But why?'

'You've forgotten? Tomorrow we complete seven years of togetherness. Exactly seven years before, you had proposed to me from your balcony.'

'Damn, you remember? I was just testing you.'

'You'd forgotten, don't lie.'

'The thing is, every date of every month with you is special for me,' he said, wrapping his arms around her.

A sudden jolt shook Avni from the beautiful dream she was having.

'Ma'am, we have reached your destination.'

Avni opened her purse and checked for the letter. It was still inside her bag.

'No problem, Bhaiya. Thank you.'

Avni paid him the fare and got out of the car. Sidharth's nana opened the door and welcomed her inside.

'Is he better?' he asked.

'Yes, slightly. He's excited about his big surprise tomorrow.' Avni sat down on a chair.

'Surprise?' Sidharth's nana asked, giving her a glass of water. He sat down beside her.

'Yes, tomorrow it will be seven years to the day he proposed to me.'

'Oh yes, I remember. It was your six-month anniversary, that day when he sneaked into your house.' Nana laughed. 'I was the one who kept his mother away from you both that night.'

Avni could recall every minute detail of that night. It was still fresh in her memory, like it had happened yesterday. Avni went inside the bedroom after dinner. Shivaansh was sound asleep. She sat beside him and gazed at him lovingly.

'Tomorrow, you'll meet your dad.' She said, kissing his forehead.

She took a hot shower and finally rested her head on the pillow. It had been a long day. She was exhausted and didn't realize when finally she dozed off. It was around 3:30 a.m. when her phone beeped. It was Sidharth's mother.

'Mom, is everything alright? Why are you calling at this hour?'

There was silence at the other end and then a loud wailing sound. 'Mom, are you okay?'

'Avni . . . Avni . . . Sidharth is no more. He's gone . . .'

Avni dropped the mobile. *This can't be happening. It's not true!* 'Mom . . . what are you . . . saying?'

'Please, come soon . . .' said Sidharth's mother.

Avni found it difficult to get out of bed. She was in shock. By the time she regained her composure, her parents had arrived to take her and Nana to the hospital. On the way, she kept thinking she was dreaming and that she would land up at the hospital and be told everything was okay.

As soon as they reached the hospital, Avni ran out of the car. Balwinder held a visibly shaken Nana and then made him sit in a wheelchair while Mona held on to Shivaansh. The walk to Sidharth's room felt like the longest walk of her life. When she finally reached the room, she opened the door with trembling hands. He was lying on the bed, lifeless. A white sheet had been draped over him. Avni broke down.

Sidharth's mother was crying uncontrollably, and when Sidharth's nana was wheeled into the room, she got up and ran to hug him. Their cries filled the room. Avni's parents tried to console them. Avni used every ounce of her energy to go close to him. He looked so much at peace. His eyes were closed. They couldn't see Shivaansh one last time. The eyes that had gazed at Avni endlessly, the eyes that always radiated love for her had closed forever.

As she looked at him one last time, she regretted not bringing Shivaansh earlier. She regretted not giving him the surprise letter she had written for him.

It was their seventh anniversary. The day he had stood in his balcony with the white board and red string lights, which now flashed in front of her eyes. I'll love you forever, he had said. Avni took his lifeless hand in hers.

Happy anniversary, dumbo.

Tears poured down her cheeks as his last words echoed in her head.

No matter what our future is, no matter what the doctors say, nothing can tear us apart. A part of me will always be you and a part of you will always be me.

Epilogue

Thirty Years Later

Death is the only constant in life. What remains behind after death are memories and their impact on our lives. Love carries those energies that can change everything in and around you. Before Avni met Sidharth, she didn't believe in love. But Sidharth changed everything. Nothing could separate them now, certainly nothing as small as death.

For the last thirty years, she had done everything she could to keep his memories alive. He would have hated to see her cry, so she lived her life the way he would have liked her to, with a smile on her face, until her last dying breath.

One morning, she passed away due to a cardiac arrest. She was survived by Shivaansh, his wife, Kritika, and their four-year-old daughter, Adya.

Shivaansh had just come back home after completing all the rituals. He stood in front of the memorial Avni had built for Sidharth after his death. The memorial had miniature statues of Sidharth and Avni holding hands, and they had been decorated with string lights and flowers. Behind it was a large photo frame of Sidharth and Avni's wedding, with the words 'Love you, forever' engraved on it. Shivaansh lit a diya, took their blessings, and prayed for Avni's soul to rest in peace.

'Mom, you were so right. Death is inevitable but the journey with your soulmate lives on forever,' he said, looking at her photo.

'I was really blessed to have a mother-in-law like her,' said Kritika. 'I could not meet Dad, but I am sure he must have been a very special person if Mom loved him so much.'

Shivaansh looked at Sidharth's photo. 'He was. I was just a year old when he left us. When I was young, my mother used to tell me so many stories about him that I always felt his presence. They were truly made for each other, and their story teaches us the meaning of real love.'

'Pappa, did Dada and Dadi love each other like the prince and princess in my book?' Adya asked.

'Beta, the prince and princess are fictional, they don't exist in the real world. But your dada and dadi were real, as was their love story.'

'Then will you tell me their story? I want to tell all my friends in school,' she said excitedly, wanting to know more about them.

'Yes, I will when you start understanding what love is.' He kissed her cheek and, turning his head towards Kritika said, 'You know, Mom always said that Dad would look into her eyes like his world resided in them. After his death, both Dadi, and Nana and Nani, told her to get married again as I was so young. But she didn't. For her, it was only Dad.'

Shivaansh looked at the frame next to their photo. It was the last letter Avni had written for Sidharth, which she had preserved for the last thirty years.

The day you came into my life, everything changed! You made me believe in love and its numerous possibilities. You made me come out of my misery when I was at my lowest. We have seen tough times together and we have come out of them. Just your presence gives me so much strength. You let me work this crazy job and manage this house and look after Shivaansh. And you never, ever question me. You never question my ability. You're just always there—on the sidelines—cheering me on, repeating over and over again that I am capable of greatness. Thank you for being my strength. Thank you for being my support system. Thank you for always telling me that nothing in this world can ever drag me down. Thank you for teaching me that love is always the answer to everything, that self-doubt and insecurity have no place in our hearts.

I couldn't be more thankful for all the ways that you have taught me the beauty of life and the wonder of love. I thank you for coming into my life and I thank God for giving yourself to me.

We all long for it, but few ever really find it, and fewer still understand it and live with it forever—true love, that is. Sidharth and Avni were undoubtedly one of those fortunate few.

~

'You know why I love you so much?' Avni asked Sidharth, holding Shivaansh when they were about to retire after his first birthday celebration.

'Because no one else wants me and no one else can ever handle me like you do,' Sidharth replied, giving her a hug.

'No, it's because you make my life so beautiful, so perfect, so complete . . . .'

'My love isn't limited to one lifetime. I will keep loving you forever.'

After Sidharth's journey ended, though they lived in two distant worlds, they were one, and now, their souls had been united again. To love and to be loved. Isn't it incredible? Two hearts, two minds, two destinies, two souls, but one feeling, one road, one journey, one ending, and true love forever!